Dear Carol,

I'm going to do it. Maybe Mom's right. And now Lee, too. I'm going to get on those braces and use them. I'm really going to try. Maybe this time it'll work. Lee wants me to try. It's important to him. I'd just about do anything he asked. I guess that's what love is all about.

Rennie

Dear Rennie,

I'm so afraid you're going to get hurt. Rennie, be careful. Lee is able-bodied. He's a walker not a gimp. He's on the other side. Don't forget it. He can be nice to you and smile and drive you home, but when it comes down to the nitty gritty, he's still on the other side. People don't cross over. They don't let you cross over either. Believe me, I know. . . .

Carol

THE
Lionhearted

by Harriet May Savitz

A SIGNET BOOK
NEW AMERICAN LIBRARY
TIMES MIRROR

COPYRIGHT © 1975 BY HARRIET MAY SAVITZ

Library of Congress Catalog Card Number: 75-6878

This is an authorized reprint of a hardcover edition published
by The John Day Company. The edition was published simul-
taneously in Canada by Fitzhenry & Whiteside Limited, Toronto.

 SIGNET TRADEMARK REG. U.S. PAT. OFF. AND FOREIGN COUNTRIES
REGISTERED TRADEMARK—MARCA REGISTRADA
HECHO EN CHICAGO, U.S.A.

SIGNET, SIGNET CLASSICS, MENTOR, PLUME AND MERIDIAN BOOKS
are published by The New American Library, Inc.,
1301 Avenue of the Americas, New York, New York 10019

FIRST SIGNET PRINTING, FEBRUARY, 1977

3 4 5 6 7 8 9

PRINTED IN THE UNITED STATES OF AMERICA

*To Lee Nauta whose lion heart beats no more . . .
and to Rosalie Hixson who continues to share
her courage and extraordinary abilities
with others.*

Contents

Rennie's World

Rain splashing on the streets, rain and summer flowers whizzing by. She and Mike riding the sleek black motorcycle, daring the wind that beat down on them, daring the summer night. Past one street, and then another, faster, faster. Suddenly, a screech, then the motorcycle somersaulting as though it were a clown. Rennie remembered the moon swinging crazily in the sky as her body spun into the air and hit the ground.

She shook her head, closing her eyes for a moment, trying to shake off the memories of that hour that had reshaped her life. She wheeled over to the desk underneath the pink-curtained bedroom window and pulled out some stationery from the drawer. Then, slowly, trying to wipe away the yesterdays she no longer wanted to remember, Rennie began a letter to her dear friend and past roommate, Carol.

Dear Carol,

I really think he knows I'm alive. Yesterday in class, Lee Snyder walked over and smiled. He even sat down in the seat next to me. It was the first time we really had a chance to talk. You know, not see you later, how's things kind of talk.

9

*But really to me, words just to me. He looked
right into my eyes and it was just the two of us
there in the middle of the class. All the other girls,
they just stared. Honestly, Carol, I felt a giggle
ride around inside me because I knew they were
watching. I know I keep writing about him. You
must actually get bored though you're too good
a friend to admit it. But it's been six weeks and
there's no one else I can tell. Who else would
believe it, that I could think I stand a chance with
one of the best-looking guys in the class. I have
to leave for school now. I'll write more later.*

Love, Rennie

*P.S. I told you there was nothing to worry
about when I started attending this school. It's
all going to be OK . . . in fact better than OK.
Just super!*

She believed it. Licking the envelope and putting it
on her desk to be mailed later, Rennie believed that
her being at Ridge High School was the best thing that
had ever happened to her since the night of the accident. Her family referred to it as "that night," when
Mike, who lived around the corner, had driven by on
his motorcycle. She hadn't asked anyone that night
whether or not she could go.

It seemed so natural to hop on the motorcycle in
back of him, to spin around, just once around the
block, while Mike showed off to his friends and neigh-
bors the new set of wheels and the excited blonde who
clung with tightened arms about his waist. Once
around was all it was supposed to be, but with the
cool rain whipping about her face, she had coaxed,
"More, Mike, more." She had been the one to be
hypnotized by the softness of the night, as they had
gone down the wide streets, darting in and out of the
night traffic. She completely forgot all the reasons why
she shouldn't be where she was, reasons like a wet

night and slick streets and reflections that fooled the eye and slid along the avenues with glossy deception.

The tires seemed so safe until they hit a corner where a light suddenly turned red and then they went crazy, losing their grip on the street. Suddenly Mike was gone. Her arms were empty, and an unending pain was licking her body. Mike had died there on a street, with strange faces peering down at him, without ever saying another word. Quickly the ambulance took her away, while Mike lay there waiting, not needing anything from anyone anymore.

After the accident, Rennie had come home from the hospital in a wheelchair. It did not turn out a temporary, "just for a while, but it will be different" kind of thing. It was for the rest of her life.

Two years ago. It had been two years ago, and still her mother and father clung to the thought that she would walk again. Endless doctors, endless tries, endless false hopes. They refused to face the fact that Rennie had faced many months ago. This was it. This was the way it was to be, and would be. Her father, a district sales manager for a cosmetics company, had been on the road more and more during the past two years. Rennie knew in her heart that his absence was due to her, to the fact that he couldn't bear to watch her slide up the steps on her backside, pull herself down to the floor when she wanted to get around without the wheelchair. All these things made him turn away, go back to whatever was out there on the road.

She wouldn't let her parents sell the house and move elsewhere. Though there were four steps to her bedroom, she fought against their moving into a ranch home, out of the neighborhood, away from her friends, from everything she had been a part of for so long. But even though they had stayed, Rennie knew she had taken a step back away from everything she had known before. And though she still lived in the same house, spoke to the same girls on the sidewalks around the neighborhood, it was very different.

If her mother minded, she didn't have time to show it. All her energies revolved around Rennie. "Try to walk, Rennie, try to walk with the braces," her mother would urge, time and time again. "At least try." Sometimes she would watch Rennie transfer quickly to the couch as though her legs might spring out from under her and begin to move on their own, but it never happened. Rennie knew her mother lived in constant hope that one day it would happen.

"Drop it." Sometimes she wanted to say that. "Forget it. Leave it alone." But she knew that her parents couldn't abandon that hope, especially her mother. Just as they both couldn't accept her as being disabled. Other people were crippled. Not Rennie. There were deformed people on the telethons, or parents active in organizations for crippled children because they had disabled offspring, but Rennie, their daughter Rennie, well, it had to be just for now . . . just for a while.

At the Rehabilitation Center it had been different. Rennie had learned to laugh again with young people of her own age who had fallen down the steps, out of trees, been in the wrong automobile seat at the wrong time — all of them sharing the bond of wheels and knowing that this was the way it was to be for the rest of their lives.

"Rennie, come on, honey, we'll be late." Her mother threw an overcoat over her shoulders and came into the room. Her hair was black, streaked with bits of gray that had just begun to show two years ago. Her mother used to laugh a lot. Rennie remembered the years when laughter was full and plenty in their home. It wasn't there as much anymore. She wished it were. She wished her mother and father could laugh and do more together. She'd feel better then. Instead they spent their time just wishing that she could walk again, and somehow this made her feel like a wedge between them and laughter.

Mrs. Jackson wheeled Rennie through the living room and down the ramp at the front door. Rennie transferred from the wheelchair into the front seat of the car, and her mother carefully folded the wheelchair and put it in the back of the car. It was a morning ritual they had followed ever since Rennie had been accepted into Ridge High School, as a result of her unwavering insistence. After the accident and being at the Rehabilitation Center, after learning about herself and her new machine, she was ready to go back to her studies. That meant returning to school. She knew it had to be Ridge High. Her mother had urged, pleaded with her to go to a special school, a school that was for the disabled. "It'll be easier," she had coaxed. "And they probably won't even let you into Ridge. You know how difficult it will be."

Carol, her roommate at the Rehabilitation Center, had been on her mother's side. Her closest confidante, Carol had later returned to her own home in the Midwest. Remembering her friend Carol, whose eyes could grow cool and distant as protection against the insensitivity of others, Rennie could see her as though she were here in the room, shaking her head and cautioning, "Don't ask for trouble, Rennie."

It was the only emotional experience she couldn't share with her friend, the only goal that they differed on. Carol had been disabled since birth. She had just gone back to the Rehabilitation Center for a couple of months to brush up on some secretarial courses. Her schooling had always been in special classrooms for special children.

Rennie didn't want it that way. She had remained stubborn, through the school board meetings and the small conferences with therapists and doctors. Ridge High School was accessible, except for three steps at the front of the school. The school had taken the position that Rennie would not be able to attend the school because of those three steps.

They had fought back and forth, Rennie refusing to believe that those steps could keep her out of the school, knowing that all she needed was someone to lift the wheelchair, and that would be that. Her persistence paid off. A local newspaperman got interested in her struggle, wrote a story in his human-interest column, and, with the pressure of the press spotlighting the issue, the school board suddenly found the three insurmountable steps surmountable. Each morning Rennie's mother drove her to school, and the janitor and one of the teachers lifted the wheelchair up the three steps. Each afternoon after school, her mother would pick her up at the bottom of the steps. The rest of the school had wide hallways, and all the classrooms were on one floor.

Even now, Rennie could hardly believe that she was attending the modern school of over three thousand students. Before the accident, she had walked to the school a hundred times with her friends, examining the classrooms, stretching out on the lawn, pretending even then, years ago, that it was her school. Even in junior high it had meant so much to her. Ridge High meant more to her now. Because she had to fight for it.

Her mother drove slowly past the familiar homes that dotted the city streets. "Rennie, your father and I want you to see Dr. Block."

Rennie looked over at her mother. Again. It was to start again. She should have realized that, as always, the uneasy silence would be followed by a new attempt to get her on her feet.

"He's supposed to be the best orthopedic doctor in the country. Rennie, he's interested in your case. Perhaps . . ."

Rennie didn't say anything. She just looked out of the window, hoping that the houses would pass faster and that school might rescue her from a decision.

The minutes passed by, and she let out her breath quietly, not wanting the slightest sound to encourage her mother to continue the conversation. Another doctor. Would they ever give up? She could tell the doctor that there was not the slightest doubt in her mind that she would never walk again. She could give it to the doctor straight that something inside you tells the truth and what it is. The truth was that she lost the ability to walk back there on the slick street two years ago, and it wasn't something that you could go back and pick up like a forgotten umbrella or a pair of gloves. She had faced the realization that there would be no sudden reprieve. A peace, a gentle acceptance had taken the place of panic.

Why was it so hard for everyone around her to believe it and learn to live with it? Why couldn't the ones she loved, those who knew her before the accident, believe it and accept it and go on from there? What was it that blinded them, that made it so difficult for them to see that she was still Rennie who loved to laugh, to share, to love? They had closed her up behind long cotton curtains. She could sense those moving, talking, busy people on the other side.

"Rennie, please don't clam up like that. We'd just like you to meet with him."

Rennie remembered a big box turtle in her neighbor's yard, which she saw last week. With strangers hovering all around him, the box turtle had tucked his neck and face, and everything that was visible, neatly, deeply inside his shell. Now here, in the car, not wanting to hurt her mother with the truth of it all, she was that box turtle, tucked deep inside herself.

"We can't give up," her mother said softly.

Number fourteen or fifteen. Rennie knew doctors as well as she knew when the peaches were ripe and just ready to drop. The doctor's predictable smile, his handshake, his X rays, his frown, were maps of past journeys that must not be traveled again. She was weary of the road because she knew where it must lead. Why didn't anyone else?

She shook her head in a silent protest as the stubbornness that had persisted during the Ridge High battle came to the surface. "I'm finished trying," she said. Her voice was low but firm as she looked at the tears that sprung into her mother's eyes. "I'm not going to see another doctor."

Her mother pulled up in front of the school. "Well, we'll see," she said. "We'll see." She kissed Rennie, with tears still wet around her cheeks.

It isn't so bad. Rennie wanted to tell her that. She wanted to put her arms around her mother and say, "Hey, it really isn't that bad at all. This wheelchair— it seems worse to you. I can see, hear and feel happiness inside me, growing every day. If you'd only give it a chance, maybe life will open up with something new and exciting. Now, this minute, it's worse for you."

The words didn't come out. The tears that she faced, the sorrowful eyes locked the words inside her. If she ever had the courage to speak out, she feared no one would believe her.

Her mother got out her wheelchair, and Rennie slid into it. They waited, as they always did, at the bottom of the three steps that seemed to hold the big school behind it, beyond Rennie's reach. Joe, the janitor, waved from the doorway and came down. Behind him, with light hair and a broad smile, was tall, broad-shouldered Lee Snyder. He walked behind her wheelchair, and she felt his strong hands rest on the chair.

Her Lee. In her mind, in her dreams, he had become that. Rennie blushed. She felt the hot flush on her face and hoped it wouldn't be noticeable. Lee had never before helped lift her up the steps. It was always a teacher and Joe.

"Hi, Mrs. Jackson, how are you?" Still smiling, he shook her hand.

She responded warmly to his greeting, quickly

wiping away the smudges left under her eyes by the recent tears. "Fine, thank you," she said. Then she touched the back of Rennie's head as though unspoken words clung to her fingertips. Saying, "I'll see you this afternoon," she hurried away to her car.

"Careful," Joe cautioned, but the wheelchair remained steady as they carried it up the steps. Joe opened the front door and Lee pushed Rennie into the hallway, crowded with students.

"OK, Rennie, you're on your own." Joe smiled good-naturedly and went into the office.

Lee stood beside the chair, his hands in his pockets, quietly looking down at her.

"Well, thanks." Rennie looked up, wishing that she could find a reason for him to stay but knowing that there wasn't one.

"You'll be OK?" he asked with a concern that caught her by surprise.

"Sure," she said, trying to reassure him.

He nodded, then walked quickly into the room across the hall. He would have been shocked if he could have read the thoughts passing through her head. Rennie sat there for a moment, realizing that her thoughts would have shocked her mother even more.

Although he helped to lift her up the steps by mere chance, she felt more strongly than ever that, before long, they would become deeply involved with each other.

Lee

Making its way noisily back and forth across the lawn, the lawn mower was gobbling up the grass. Lee Snyder made zigzagging designs over the lawn trying to break up the monotony of the job as the heat of the afternoon sun dotted him with perspiration. This was the last day of his summer job, and it always seemed as though the grass was the longest on that day. In September the grass on all the lawns would grow long at the same time, and all the customers wanted the mowing done the same day.

The phone would start ringing early on these cool fall days, and his mother, with a worried look on her face, would say, "Lee, you'll never get them all done." Every year she'd worry, and he'd hug her and laugh her worries away.

Only this fall it was different. It would be the last time that he would take summer mowing jobs. Lee sat down on the lawn and wiped his head with a handkerchief. The Bensons were nice people, and he had known them since he was five, when they had moved into a new neighborhood where trees looked like shrubs and lawns were covered with more mud than grass.

But changes had reshaped the neighborhood during

the past thirteen years. Houses had multiplied, and fields had sprouted shopping centers. Expressways over the rolling hills facilitated journeys into town. There was a bowling alley now where the old pig farm had been, where the Bensons and Zawiskis and a lot of other people had moved in. The trees were tall now and the grass firm. Lee had depended on that fast-growing grass to bring in a steady income during the past five summers.

He looked at his watch. In another hour he would be due at Mr. Dansick's tie shop. The sweat rolling down his back momentarily cooled him. Lee got up, stretched, tied the handkerchief around his forehead and started the mower back up.

Mr. Dansick didn't like anyone coming late for work at the tie ship. He treated the racks of ties as if they were diamond watches, and Lee knew how he felt about employees who didn't have the same respect for the ties or for the clock that sat directly above the front door of the shop.

"Nobody cares about his job anymore," Mr. Dansick would often confide in him on the two nights a week and Saturday morning, when he worked there part time. "Most kids today don't take pride in their work."

Lee didn't disagree with him. Many of his friends worked at ice cream stands or in hamburger drive-ins. But it was just putting in time. They didn't really care about what they were doing or even if they did it right.

Mr. Dansick cared. He cared about the ties as he'd unpack them, straighten and hang them with matching designs, in the right groups, the best ones on the bottom, "to make the customer search a little. This way they'll buy a few of the not so good ones on top." All one-dollar ties, but Mr. Dansick acted as though they were worth twenty dollars each and treated his customers as if they were a rich clientele.

The lawn mower led Lee around the flower garden

and then up and down the front of Mrs. Benson's lawn. He turned off the mower, raked the grass and piled it in the wheelbarrow. This is the last time, Mrs. Benson, he thought as he dumped the grass in the woods adjoining their backyard. Next year you'll have to get yourself another boy to mow the lawn. Next year he would be away at college in Michigan, and the Bensons and the factory that bellowed smoke down the hill near the steel works, and the Mall—all of it would remain here.

Lee pushed the lawn mower home, parked it in the garage and went in the back door. He was dirty and his blond hair was dark from perspiration. He grabbed a clean pair of trousers folded neatly on the dryer and ran up the steps into the kitchen.

"Hey, Mom, put a fast sandwich on." Without waiting for her answer, he ran up the stairs to his bedroom, threw his dirty clothes on the floor and started the shower in the bathroom. His mother's voice caught up with him.

"Rush, rush, rush. How much time do you have?" she called from the kitchen.

"A half-hour," he answered. Then the water spilled into his ears and drowned his eyes, as the shower made him forget the grass, the hot sun and the wheelbarrows. The water streaming down on his head felt like waves rushing over him, as if he were down at the shore again. Those times at the shore, when he used to catch the waves with his father, caring about nothing but catching the waves and riding with them into the shore.

There was more to do now than ride waves. Since his dad had died three years ago, his life had been hurled into high speed. Lee opened the bureau drawers and pulled out some underwear. His clothes, like a tiny train, lay scattered about his feet. He glanced at the picture of his father, smiling warmly, on the top of his bureau, and he stopped buttoning his shirt for a moment and looked back at it. It bothered him that he couldn't remember his father's voice. Many times as he would look at the picture and try very hard to recapture the memory of his dad's voice, he wondered why they had never recorded any of his father's conversations. But they had taken plenty of pictures.

Minutes ticked by as Lee stood there remembering the good times. But somewhere in the memories, like a fog slipping in on a clear night, was the unforgettable picture of that night, the night his father had awakened, gone to the bathroom and died. There in the bathroom, alone on the cold hard floor, he had died of a stroke. Lee wondered during the months that followed what his dad had felt—just two doors down from Lee's bedroom—helpless, alone, with a split-second tornado filling his head and knowing, or not knowing, what was to follow. Lee's eyes blurred momentarily as he touched the picture.

Quickly, he got into his trousers and brushed his hair.

"Honestly," said his mother, as she came into the room, not bothering to knock, "look at this place. You're just a maniac when you rush around like that."

"It's OK," he said. "I'll get it together." Quickly he gathered the clothes from the floor and threw them into the hamper. "Come on," he said, putting his arm around her, "stop yelling at your boy and feed me."

They walked down the stairs, a closeness between them that had deepened since the death of his father. Lee liked his mother. If she weren't his mother, he would have picked her as a friend. He had felt that way about his dad, too.

"How's the job going?" Lee sat down at the kitchen table and hurriedly began to eat his sandwich.

Mrs. Snyder took the milk out of the refrigerator and shrugged. "It's not the tax season yet—so we're not too busy. But the days still rush by."

Lee was pleased that his mother had to go to work.

Though his father had left a sizable insurance fund, the years following his death saw prices climbing steadily, and they both knew that their savings would not be enough for the future that lay ahead. Because his mother had worked on and off during their marriage, helping his father out as a statistical typist, it was easy for her to find a well-paying job. But over and above the money that the job brought in, Lee was glad that each morning she had to get up and go to work among people. This helped fill the lonely hours that had left their mark around the creases of her eyes and created a slight stoop in the shoulders that weren't held quite as straight anymore.

"Got to run." Lee glanced at the clock. "I'll be a little late tonight. I've got a date with Jo."

"Just be careful driving," his mother cautioned. But behind her remark were the unspoken words, "It's just you and me now, Lee."

Thoughts about Jo Dutton and her soft body stayed with him all the way to the tie shop. Mr. Dansick looked at his watch as Lee rushed in.

"A new order just got here," he said excitedly, pointing to a stack of boxes at the far corner of the shop.

"OK, Mr. Dansick." Lee tried to calm the old man down. "You take care of the customers, and I'll take care of these." He bent down, his long body still sore from Mrs. Benson's lawn. He ripped open the cardboard boxes. Flashing colors in stripes and dots spilled out of one box after the other as Lee grabbed empty hangers and filled them with long cloth daggers.

The three hours' work at the tie shop went quickly. Lee had lost count of the stripes, how many blues and oranges he had lined up when Mr. Dansick finally came over, with a satisfied look on his face.

"Good . . . good boy." Mr. Dansick surveyed the hanging rows of ties, his face showing his pleasure.

Lee liked him. He liked the way he took pride in the little shop, treating each customer as if he were a relative. He was in awe of the reserve of strength in the seventy-year-old man, the way he could put in a full day, though he could have been collecting social security checks and living in some resort. Yet here he was, with the success of the tie shop uppermost in his mind and standing on his feet ten, sometimes twelve hours a day.

"Mr. Dansick, don't you ever think of retiring?" Lee asked him as they locked up.

Mr. Dansick's eyes grew serious, then frightened. "And do what?" he asked. "Sit with all the old people and compare social security checks? Dunk in the water and nap and then dunk again?" He patted Lee on the shoulder, and for a second, it had the same touch as his father—warm, light, definite. "To some people, retirement is heaven. To me, it's death. If I'm going to be waiting to die, I'd rather work while I'm waiting." The front door of the shop clicked closed on the conversation.

Lee left Mr. Dansick in the parking lot and drove toward Jo and the ice cream parlor where she worked. She still had on the little white skirt with a curtained apron, and her face was flushed with excitement as she stood waiting in the parking lot.

"Hop in." He patted the spot next to him and she slid in, her thighs warm against his leg. "Busy tonight?" He could see, through the shop window, the crowds just getting out from the Friday night movies. "All that ice cream." He laughed. "I think you have most on your face." She had a smudge on her nose, and he wiped it off as he drove. She cuddled closer. "I don't even want to mention ice cream," she said, her forehead creasing into a frown. "I hate that job. I hate the ice cream and the customers who want everything right away. The whole bit."

He listened to the list of hates that Jo was piling up. She usually ended up hating everything she started, and he wondered why. Her dark black hair offset her excited blue eyes, and she was very pretty. Perhaps he felt that talking did not become her. Her mouth was just the right red, even without lipstick, now curled in anger as she recounted the evening and the fight with her boss.

"He said, 'Jo, you're not waiting on the customers fast enough,' and here I was with two sundaes balanced on the tray and a steak sandwich to go."

They pulled up at Eagle's Peak. He turned off the motor and caught her mouth somewhere between the banana split and she "might never go back to work again." The words stopped. Their bodies talked. Only the sound of the leaves at Eagle's Peak worked their way through the car. Other than that, it was quiet.

She smelled of lemon. "You smell so good," Lee said.

Jo giggled and moved closer and the lemon fragrance drifted up his nostrils and warmed him.

"I haven't seen you all week," she said in between murmurs. Her hands crossed lightly over his shirt and around his neck.

"Hmm." Lee closed his eyes and leaned back against the seat. "Been mowing all the lawns in the world"— he curled closer—"and then in between, there's the tie shop."

"Work, work. Don't you ever get tired of running from place to place?" Jo pulled back from him. "I mean, you don't have time for anything anymore."

By anything, he knew she meant Eagle's Peak and this. He took her back in his arms, and she seemed to melt into his chest. An ache crept through his body. He had never told her he loved her. Jo had never asked. There were no promises, no commitments, no talk of tomorrow.

He sighed, and Jo mistook it for passion. "Do you want me?" she asked, and the moonlight spun her hair about her like a silver web and her voice, soft and warm, no longer full of "hate yous" touched him.

He pulled her head down and kissed her again, mostly because he wanted a chance to think, as he was actually wondering about that . . . whether he wanted her, and he also wondered how he could be thinking about it at a time like this.

"Are you into her pants?" had been the big question in the locker room at gym, and he had laughed because he knew plenty of the guys at school had wished for the pleasure with Jo.

Somehow his mind wouldn't stay where it was supposed to tonight. It went from the locker room to the school library and then down the front steps to a girl with green eyes and a smile that seemed both real and challenging.

"Do you know Rennie Jackson?" he asked suddenly.

Jo backed away, and then she laughed. "If you had mentioned any other girl right now, I would have slapped your face." He knew what she meant. "Yeah, I see her around. She's that crippled kid."

He felt his neck grow hot. It always did when he got angry. He didn't know why he was angry now.

"Why, are you playing Good Samaritan or something? I heard you carried her up the steps today."

Again silence. Lee played with the steering wheel in front of him. "I just don't remember seeing her that often before," he said.

"Well, she sort of keeps to herself. You know, I guess there's so little she can do, anyway."

"I wonder what happened to her. You know, how she got in that chair."

"Took a fast ride with a guy whose number was up," Jo shot back, her patience thinning. "They both were tossed off the motorcycle."

Lee thought about Rennie, laughing, that long blonde hair letting the wind take it, loving the speed. She would have loved that speed. It still showed in her eyes. The picture of her being scrambled up in a lot of black metal stayed with him. But even that hadn't taken away the look from her eyes. He saw it today, that daring look that seemed to defy the wheelchair she was in.

The scent of lemon came closer. He stirred. Her hands brought him back to the pleasures of Eagle's Peak.

"Lee, make love to me," she said at last.

He turned toward her and his body answered. What the heck. It was better than a hot fudge sundae.

On the Outside

Bess was on the outer fringe. As she sat in the classroom, her elbow pressing into the desk, her chin resting lazily on her hand, she knew somewhere in the class there was an inner circle. She wasn't sure where a circle like that began or how to step inside it. She just knew she wasn't a part of it.

Long hair, twisting this way and that, blended before her, as eager hands fluttered in the air, begging for the teacher's attention. Boys sat beside her, in front of her, whispering to one another, sharing jokes and making plans for the hours after school. Most of the time, she felt as though she didn't exist to anyone in the classroom. She could have been a window shade flapping against the fall breeze or a part of the leaves that were falling on the ground just outside the window.

One thing was certain. Even if she felt she was invisible, this was by no means true.

Far from it. "Hey, Fatty," they called to her and laughed. Bess would laugh with them, remembering her mother's words. "Bess, being fat is one strike against you. Being nasty is two." So she tried not to be nasty. She tried to remember that the extra weight she carried around with her all the time was enough to intimidate friendship or even romance.

Bess laughed and smiled and tried to understand more and more lately. When girls faded away into crowds and left her standing alone, she'd say to herself, "Well, you can't win them all," though saying it didn't help. When a boy's eager eye caught the girl behind her, the emptiness she felt inside would tug like a faint pain, just remind her of what she dreamed could happen, but she'd take a deep breath, an extra slice of cake, and assure herself that it would be different someday.

And when the others around her ribbed her and joked lightly, the small wounds that bled inside bled silently. Bess, on schedule, would shake her long red hair and joke away the hurt. "Bess, you're always so cheerful. I bet it's true, what they say about fat people. You know, they're always so happy."

Bess didn't answer her classmates truthfully. The truth might have embarrased them. It even embarrased her. The fact was that she spent many days and nights in her room crying because of the lonely walks home, because of the lonely nights that only brought promises that nothing would change tomorrow; this fact was the wedge that kept her on the outside of the circle.

She had tried everything to take off weight. No snacks, potatoes or bread. Walk away from the cakes after supper. "No, thank you," on seconds. "Just small firsts, please." She was always conscious that the next biteful, the next frustrated moment that led to the eating spree would only add and add to the helplessness she felt already.

Bess glanced now and then at the blackboard, her brown eyes hazy under dark lashes. The hard wooden seat under her felt small and uncomfortable as did the desk behind which she crowded. She shifted her weight in the chair, looking lazily around at her classmates.

The teacher, pacing back and forth in front of her desk, reminded her of a sleek panther, sleek and slim and ready to strike with questions.

Bess knew of a stack of questions, custom-made questions that she could depend on being asked daily at some point and every day in the future. "Why are you so fat? Is it a glandular problem? Were you fat as a baby? Don't you really want to lose weight?" She had been asked such personal questions by people she knew and people who didn't know her at all, as though the massiveness of her body gave everyone permission to probe into it. Sometimes an aunt or uncle would say, with a tone of disgust, "Bess, there's no excuse for your being so heavy. You're really a very pretty girl."

Bess had tried to find that pretty girl in the mirror many times. At night, with Puff, her cat, looking on in bewilderment, she would stand there in front of the long mirror attached to her closet door, and look. The long red hair would hang down in soft waves almost showing off for her. The big eyes would stare back with a clear brilliance. The nose, the mouth, the cheeks with a slight border of freckles, all added up to a face, a nice face. But then came the frame, like a punch line at the end of a joke, a disastrous punch line that made the story fall flat on its face. Wide, sexless, remote from any appeal, her body always filled the mirror with its lack of glamour.

Most of the time, she felt like a weed, off to the side of a beautiful flower garden, watching the blossoms, full of color, being sniffed and wanted and picked.

There was a boy down the block, long and skinny, with the kindest laughing blue eyes. They even laughed when his face was set without a smile. She thought of Josh, sitting there as she doodled with her pencil and lost the teacher's words until they seemed but a whisper. She watched the panther busy herself writing an assignment on the blackboard. Bess let her mind drift back to Josh. He had moved into her neighborhood a year

ago, and his kind eyes were the first thing she looked
for when she walked to school in the morning. He
liked her, the kind of liking that she felt after school
when no one was around—the way one enjoys a comfortable pair of shoes. But she was tempted to have
told him, even this morning when he stopped her on
the way to school, that she wanted to be enjoyed like
hot peppers and pizzas and the first fall football game.

"Going to the grocery store?" he'd ask.

There seemed always to be a reason why they should
stop and talk. Words came easily there on the corner
waiting till dinner time, or early in the morning as he
went to meet his friends. She wondered if he noticed
that she couldn't stop smiling when she looked at him,
or that her freckles danced all over the place with
pleasure.

But he never walked with her. Never in school, or
out of it. He never asked her to the dances or to the
movies. Bess knew why and almost didn't expect it of
him. But she couldn't help wondering why he couldn't
care for all of her, everything that was part of her. He
was no different from the rest. They'd pat her on the
back and say, "Hey, Bess, you're great . . . what a
personality." Always the haunting remarks, "Bess,
you make me laugh like no one can." But none of them,
none of those she'd make laugh would walk with her
either. Not really the kind of walking when it's spring
and the sun is hot and the best of dreaming is all
around you, or walking through the winter snow and
confiding quietly to a best friend.

If she had a best friend, she could tell her about
the doctors she had been sent to, who had poked and
jabbed and frowned and sent her to a diet camp. She
had lost thirty pounds at the camp and returned to
school, where no one seemed to notice. So she put
back forty pounds immediately, because no one would
notice that, either, and something inside her growled

with hunger. But hunger for what? A best friend might have been able to answer that.

"It's up to you," the last doctor had said. "Bess, there are all kinds of pills and diets, but it is up to you and what you want out of life. If you want to be fat all your life and you can cope with what it'll bring, then it's your privilege." She had been pleased with him for that, for giving her the privilege of making the choice.

Yet what kind of privilege was it, not to be able to fit behind your own desk, to cringe in dressing rooms while salesgirls looked at you with pitying eyes? Gym always proved to be a dismal experience. How she had huddled and huddled, time after time, under the shower trying to reduce in size what could not be diminished, and took on larger proportions when wet. To the girls around her, it was just shower time, and they would run in and out, barely dry, wet hair clinging to the school clothes. But for her, it was an ordeal that few others could understand. Perhaps they laughed behind her back—perhaps they were glad that her body didn't belong to them.

Sometimes in a flash of honesty she could pinpoint the reason for her overeating. Her mother—so petite that it seemed hard to believe that Bess belonged to her—looked at her with a sadness that veiled her eyes. But her mother's eyes hadn't been sad this morning. They were set with determination as she had placed the wedding invitation before Bess on the kitchen table. Bess had been waiting for that invitation, for it meant a trip to Washington to see her favorite cousin. Somewhere between the orange juice and the toast, her mother had said quietly, "You'll go only if you lose thirty pounds between now and the time of the wedding."

Though several hours had passed, Bess still could not believe her mother's words. Two months to lose thirty pounds. Her eyes closed as she tried to figure out how

much that would add up to per week. When she opened
her eyes again, they were cold with anger. An ultima-
tum. The wedding was just another bribe, piled up on
top of all the other ultimatums and bribes, like tiny
blocks, only this last block had started the whole tower
swaying and it wouldn't stop until it fell. She was
finished doing it their way. She was through with the
diet pills, the restrictions, the lectures and most of all
the threats. Hang her cousin's wedding.

The bell rang. Bess looked up at the clock. Three-
fifteen. Quickly, she gathered up her books, remembering that she and the school choir were due to sing at
the Children's Rehabilitation Center. She hurried to
the bus and edged her way through the other girls.

Thoughts of the solo she was to sing kept her
preoccupied during the ride to the center. She felt most
confident when she was singing or playing the piano
at home. Somehow, as her fingers traveled over the
keys, or she hummed a song, life seemed to settle
down, become less choppy and uncertain. The other
girls began to hum on the bus, singing school songs.
Bess joined them, her voice dominating the others,
like the clear bell ringing at the corner church.

The bus stopped at a sprawling ranch-type building.
Amid nurses and helpers the girls piled off the bus and
were led into the house. Bess observed how wide the
inside of the school was, with five or six moving
wheelchairs in the hallway. There was very little furni-
ture, and it was spaced in such a way that the children
in wheelchairs were able to get around freely. Wheelchairs zigzagged all around them, crowding into the
room where the choir had already assembled. There
were some very young children and some of Bess's age.
She noticed how many of the young people in the room
had thin legs, but strong and muscular arms. Something
inside her responded to the expression in their eyes.
Perhaps it was because they looked at her, and everyone else, with the common denominator of acceptance.

The rest of the girls from the choir moved about awkwardly. Their inexperience in dealing with a room filled with wheelchairs showed clearly on their faces. And, mixed with the confusion, there was an underlying current of pity. Bess's reaction was entirely different. A sense of wonderment bubbled inside of her at the laughter and activity throughout the room. The sensitivity that others admonished her for, with "Bess, you cry too easily" or "Bess, you take offense too often," led her to believe that this time she was among friends.

The choir from Ridge High School stood on the platform, and voices blended into harmony that filled the winding hallways. One song after the other, as applause from the audience inspired the choir to sing its best. Bess felt an elation she had never experienced before.

And then it was time for her solo. The room grew hushed. She sang "Ava Maria" with such heart that she felt herself tremble. She didn't know what it was like not to walk. But she knew what it was like to be on the outside. So she sang for herself, for all those watching her, who spent their lives on the outer fringe. A silence fell over the children, who moments before had been chattering excitedly, as Bess's song reached those for whom she was singing. At the end of her performance, a joyous applause that went on and on thundered through the room.

Later, cookies and punch were served. Bess was about to go over to the cookie dish when a hand touched her. She turned around. A girl, about her own age, smiled up at her. "You have a beautiful voice. I just had to tell you."

Bess turned away from the cookies. "Thank you." Her face grew red as she shoved her hair off her shoulders. The girl in front of her looked familiar. She knew she had seen her before. There was a moment's silence between them.

"I'm Rennie Jackson. I go to Ridge High."

"Oh, yes." Bess turned around and put some cookies on a plate. She felt embarrassed that she hadn't remembered Rennie. Rennie was the first and only wheelchair student at Ridge High. There had been quite a bit of excitement on that first day when she had appeared. But then gradually, as the months went by, Rennie and the wheelchair didn't seem as obvious. Bess remembered seeing the wheelchair and the long blonde hair, but she never really remembered looking at Rennie's face until now.

"Would you like a cookie?" she offered.   Rennie shook her head.

"No, thanks. Hey, you have some time before the bus comes?"

"Yes, about a half-hour."

"Great, Come on, I'll show you around."

They went through the long hallways slowly, and Rennie pointed to the different rooms and explained what was taught in each classroom.

"How come you're here today?" Bess asked.

"This is my alma mater." Rennie brought her into a room. "This used to be my old bedroom. I stayed here for a while until I was admitted to Ridge High. I just come back now and then to help with the younger kids."

Rennie slid out of the chair and onto the bed. "I know the girl who has this room now. It's OK. Come on, sit down."

Bess sat down next to her. She didn't even know Rennie could sit without the wheelchair holding her up.

"Ridge High is great," Rennie said, smiling broadly. "I just love it."

"Me, too," Bess answered. "I've been going there for two years. Every minute's been a ball." She didn't feel she was lying. Nothing bad had really happened. She was not ready to admit to Rennie that nothing good happened either and that nothing could be a catastrophe all by itself. Bess found out that, while she was taking courses for college, Rennie was taking business administration courses. That's why they had not seen much of each other.

"I'd like to get a job as a secretary. What do you want to be?" Rennie looked toward her for an answer.

Bess wanted to say, "Thin" but instead shrugged and answered, "I only wish I knew."

Bess found it easy to talk to Rennie, and the two girls lost themselves in conversation until the bus was ready to go back. Rennie transferred over to her wheelchair and rode with Bess to the bus stop.

"My mother's picking me up," Rennie said. "These school buses weren't built with wheelchairs in mind." And then she smiled. "See you at school Monday?"

Bess stood on the steps of the bus, suddenly wishing that Rennie could have driven home with her. "I'll look for you at lunch," she said, and went to the back of the bus, not feeling alone this time, as she had on the trip here. She waved to Rennie from the window. The smile was still on Rennie's face.

But Bess knew all about smiles. She smiled and laughed a lot, too. She was the easygoing good-natured Bess. But there were times after school, in her room, when the shades were drawn and the radio played and no one but Puff her cat snuggled next to her, that the tears came because the laughter was false and the smile was paste.

She wondered. Was it like that for Rennie, too?

Wheeling It

Rennie slid out of bed and into the wheelchair. She looked out of the window, up at the gray sky filled with the promise of rain. It didn't help her depressed mood. It had begun last night, just like a heavy blanket smothering all thoughts of laughter, and was hanging over her this morning. A low, heavy feeling that made everything, normally easy, seem like an effort.

Rennie wheeled over to the closet and went through her wardrobe. Her parents had lowered the racks for her so that she could easily reach her clothes without asking anyone to help her. This morning she felt she needed help in even deciding what to wear. Everything looked either worn, dirty or overused.

She frowned as she looked toward the back of the closet. The braces were still there, standing against the wall, though she should have known that there was no reason for them to be taken away. Rennie looked at them thoughtfully. They were always there as a reminder. Today she didn't need any reminders. Today, the grayness of the day, the hint of rain, brought it all back, vividly, as though it were to happen again and again.

Following the accident, the weeks had been a procession of hospitals, doctors, a rehabilitation center, physical therapists, and then the braces. At the time, it had seemed almost comical to lie flat on a piece of paper and see the doctor drawing an outline of her body. It could have been a game, a tracing game, but it wasn't. She wasn't a little girl tracing animals and trees with her friends. She was the one being traced, so that her braces would fit her body.

The doctors took her shoe size, her calf measurements, measured the distance of her knee from her hip, and from the ankle to the knee. Waist measurements were taken, and she had watched, like a sleepwalker, as pelvic measurements were added to the list. They knew how many inches there were from her hip joint to the height on her back, where she stopped feeling. Based on all the measurements, she was fitted with a corset. Wide leather straps circled her pelvis, and pads lay across her knees. The braces, after many weeks of adjusting, had been completed. And from the moment she wore them, she felt locked in.

A physical therapist was assigned to her, and he set up a program for her. He was gentle and understanding. He tried to teach her how to fall properly, how to fall on her forearm bending her arms, opening her hands so that she didn't jar her shoulders. She remembered his soft words, like those of a ski instructor explaining to a new student on the slopes how to toss his body from the skis and avoid serious injury. "Hands down," the therapist had cautioned. "Use them as a cushion so that your arms are between your chest and the floor. This will prevent your face from hitting flat."

She hadn't really needed the instructions, because, even then, she had no intention of wearing the braces. Physical therapists, orthopedic doctors, state clinics, X rays, the brace department—she had traveled the whole route, knowing all along that she was on the wrong road. It was wrong for her. Maybe not for others who found braces the best alternative. But during the months she was being fitted and refitted, she became convinced that the wheelchair was her source of freedom.

Rennie closed the closet door, shutting out the braces. She envied the determination of many of the disabled who suffered their discomfort of the braces, and yet wore them with ease.

Rennie wheeled into the bathroom and began brushing her teeth. She had to move her legs sideways because her parents had enclosed the bottom of the sink so that the hot pipes wouldn't burn her legs. She couldn't feel those pipes. She couldn't feel a lot of things around her body. Her legs and her stomach kept her aware of the danger of being hurt because she couldn't feel the warning of pain.

Today, perhaps because the dark clouds outside carried memories with them, the wheelchair seemed a heavy load to carry. She knew there would be days like this. Though she smiled easily most of the time, there were days and moments like this when the past came back to haunt her as though it were a story she had read about someone else.

She got dressed, then slid out of her wheelchair and down the couple of steps to the wheelchair, which stood open at the bottom of the steps. It was mostly during rainy days—when the sun didn't help her along —that her mind would taunt her with "ifs." If she hadn't gone on the motorcycle, if she hadn't urged Mike to go on, if it hadn't rained, if she had only done something different, used up the hours sleeping or going for a walk . . . then she wouldn't have gone with Mike, and her life would have been different. The "if days" meant trouble, because she couldn't change what had happened.

She wheeled into the living room and put on her coat.

"Honey, I'll be with you in a minute. No breakfast?"

Rennie shook her head. "Not hungry. Look, forget about driving me this morning. I don't have any books to carry. I'll wheel over."

Her mother hurried out of the kitchen. "Don't be silly, Rennie. It's going to rain and it'll take you close to a half-hour to wheel over to the school."

"I'm early," Rennie persisted. "I'll make it."

"Please, just wait a minute . . . "

Rennie had opened the door.

"But the rain . . . "

"If it rains, I'll get wet, just like anyone else who walks in the rain." She didn't want her mother's morning to start this way. She knew it would be easier just to go along and drive to school. It would bring the smile back to her mother's face and make her day a little better. But she couldn't today. She needed room to breathe, to push her frustrations out of her, to move her arms and feel that she was taking herself somewhere. She needed time to forget the braces in the closet and the "ifs" around her life before the school bell rang.

Rennie wheeled down the ramp and onto the sidewalk. Her mother still half-walked, half-ran behind her.

"Please, Rennie. It's too long a distance."

But Rennie waved her off. "Then it's about time I learned if it's too long or not. Don't worry, I'll send up a flare if I need a ride."

She wheeled down the block against the grayness of the morning. There were very few familiar faces walking this morning. Most of the students went on the school bus. Once she had questioned the principal about the possibility of a bus with a ramp, but the principal had said, "Rennie, we can't accommodate everyone. We couldn't possibly get special equipment on the bus for one person."

She had wanted to answer that, perhaps if the buses were more accessible, there would be more disabled students going to their school, but then she wasn't sure that he wanted more disabled students.

Cars went by slowly, cars with familiar faces at side windows, and now and then someone would honk a horn and wave. Rides were offered to her, but this morning she turned them down.

No, she didn't want a ride. She just wanted to work her way out of the stillness inside her, out of the frustration that was nagging at her. She tilted her wheelchair up and hopped the curb. There were no ramps to make the ride easier, and she made a mental note to talk to one of the commissioners about ramping the curbs. If they asked, "Just for you Rennie?" then she might remind them that there were other disabled, and elderly people, and pregnant women who might benefit from the ramping. The thought of such a project excited her and began to blot out the early-morning blues.

A light mist fell upon her face and licked her lips as she wheeled across the street and hopped another curb. The school was just coming into sight. Though it was still several blocks away, a small glow of pride swept through her. She knew now she could make it. She didn't have to be driven if she didn't want to. That knowledge of independence brightened her face. In nice spring days, she could just wheel out of the front door. The fog began to lift from her thoughts, and the day took on a new turn.

"Hey, where you rushing to?" Lee caught up with her.

"Oh, I didn't realize I was wheeling so fast," Rennie answered, a little out of breath.

"From back there, you looked like you were in a race. Up one curb and down the other. When I saw you tilt that chair, I shut my eyes. Did you wheel all the way from your house?"

"You bet I did," she said with pride.

"Well, slow down now a little, because I can't

walk that fast. Besides, we still have plenty of time."

Rennie turned the wheels a little slower. "It's good practice wheeling like this. Sometimes I go out for track-and-field events in wheelchair sports. I usually enter the races. So wheeling this distance is a great workout for me."

"How do you like the school?" he asked.

"It's quite a big place to get around in. It's great."

"You're graduating soon, aren't you?"

"This June, hopefully."

She didn't want to think about it. Though she had seen him from a distance often and dreamed about their friendship, there had been little chance this year to even begin to get to know him. And here he was talking about June and graduation.

"Are you going to go away to school?"

"Yup. Michigan State. Probably take up accounting."

Again a small note of defeat rang somewhere in the distance.

Why should it matter? Halfway across the country. But it did matter. He would be out of their town and out of her life. Though he had never really stepped into it. But while he was in school, there was always a possibility of running into him, in the halls or at the front steps, and getting to know him better.

"You must be tired," he said as they reached the front steps of the school. "Wait, I'll call Joe. We'll get you up the steps."

Once inside the hall, Ronnie let her body sag for a moment in the chair. She was tired. The muscles in her arms began to relax, and her whole body tried to regain its strength.

"Do you want me to wheel you to class?" Lee asked, noticing her sudden fatigue and the whiteness of her face.

"No, thank you," Rennie said a little haughtily. She didn't like to be wheeled. Even when her arms ached like today, she would refuse unless the situation was urgent. "I can manage," she said, swinging her chair toward her locker.

Lee stopped her chair for a second and knelt down so that his clear eyes were looking right into hers. His arms rested on the arms of the wheelchair, so close that they were almost touching hers, as though he were enclosing her in his arms.

"You're some girl, Rennie." His voice was husky as he spoke. "I've never met anyone like you," he added and then, abruptly, he stood up. "I'll see you around," he said. He disappeared, swallowed up by all the other faces.

During English class, only part of Rennie was there. The other part was still feeling Lee's arms on her wheelchair, hearing his voice, wanting to touch his hands.

She didn't see him the rest of the day. She looked for him, trying not to be too obvious about it. "Hey, Rennie, how you doin'?" Familiar faces, some friends waving, and "Do you need any help?" were things she often saw and heard as she wheeled down the hall. She was grateful that so many in the school were fond of her.

And yet she didn't delude herself. Carol had warned her so many times during those nights when walking still seemed a part of her life that she couldn't give up. "People will be nice to you," she had written, "as long as you stay in your place. Don't cause a ripple. Don't try to take a chunk that they think you don't deserve."

She had been puzzled by the bitterness that Carol had inside her, the feeling that she had to stay in her place. What place? Two years had taught her a lot, but she didn't know the answer to what place she belonged, and the words continued to haunt her.

She was in front of her locker at the end of school, and a fatigue that she had been fighting all day took over. Lee walked over with a couple of his friends chattering behind him.

"Ready to pack up? And don't tell me you're going to wheel home."

"No," Rennie said. "I've had enough. Though some day, I might try it both ways." Lee saw that determined look in her eyes.

Someone said, "Hey, let's go over to Pat's for some ice cream."

"Sounds like a good idea," Lee answered. "How about some ice cream for a tired athlete? I could drive you home from the shop," he said as he turned toward Rennie.

She wanted to. "Yes" was on her lips and nearly out of her mouth when she remembered Pat's doorway, the thin doorway that everyone joked about and slid by. The doorway that had kept her and her parents out one night when they had gone there and all three of them had turned away, surprised and disappointed.

She wanted to tell him, "The doorway's not wide enough for my chair . . . or could you go somewhere that I can get into?" But she wasn't sure where that was. She stopped herself. Perhaps it was pride, perhaps it was that place that Carol had warned her about. Could any of them understand anyone not being able to enter an ice cream shop because of the width of the door?

"No, thanks," she said finally. "I really am a little tired today. And my mother is due to pick me up. Maybe next time."

Lee put his hand on her shoulder. "Don't try to do it all in one day, tiger," he said. And she wanted to tell him, then, she could do it all in one day, as much as he could, if she didn't have so many obstacles in her way.

Suddenly she was angry at the curbs she had to hop, at the doorways she couldn't get through. But she smiled at Lee through her anger and watched him as he joined all his waiting friends.

Rennie sat there for a while after he left, straightening out her locker, not wanting her mother to see her return in the same mood she had left. She had tried and tried hard to turn on the day. She had failed, except for a glimmer, now and then, to turn it around at all.

Rennie wheeled over to the entrance of the school and waited for her mother's car to pull up. Joe wheeled her down the steps.

"Hi!" Bess, her hair forming almost a red sunbeam around her face, ran over to her, as Joe went back into the school.

"Hi," Rennie said and took hold of her hand. "I was looking for you today." She had been, when she wasn't looking for Lee. She had thought about Bess and hoped to see her again.

"How could you miss me?" Bess joked.

Rennie let it go by.

"You waiting for someone?"

"Yes, for my mother," Rennie answered; "She picks me up here every day. How about you?"

"No. I don't live far from here. I usually walk home." Bess pointed down the winding hill leading from the school. "It's a nice walk, just inside the school limit, so the bus won't take me."

A slow trickle of rain began to fall and wet the leaves on the ground. The sound of it, like tiny icicles dropping, circled them.

"Why don't you wait around and we'll drop you home." Rennie put her coat over her head.

"You can go upstairs and wait in the hall," Rennie suggested as the rain grew heavier. "When you're in a wheelchair, you sort of get used to things like this." Rennie tried joking, as the water trickled onto her nose and down her coat.

Bess stood there for a second, hesitating. Then she

knelt down, her huge frame squatting, trying to become smaller. She spread Rennie's coat over the top of her head, the two of them taking shelter like little sparrows caught in a rainstorm.

"It's OK," she said. "I'll wait here with you."

It was a cloud-laden day. There was no reason to think that it was a day that would bring good things. But there, under the coat, with rain dripping down around them, Rennie felt it was turning out to be just the right kind of day . . . to find a friend.

Party Plans

They sat at the archery range, enthralled by what was going on in front of them. Bess sat on the grass next to Rennie's wheelchair.

"Boy, can you see me standing in that line in front of everyone?"

Rennie laughed. "Come on, Bess. You said you'd try."

Bess stood up, hesitating. Perhaps it wasn't such a good idea. This was part of the campaign to get her to the wedding. Her mother had decided that she needed to participate in a sport. Bess had turned down tennis, swimming and hockey. Only archery seemed to fascinate her. She had watched the archers after school, the graceful arrows twisting through the air, as though they had eyes to find the target. But Bess was more impressed by the fact that archery seemed to demand the least physical energy than she was by its beauty.

She really didn't care about the wedding anymore. It was no longer a matter of losing weight or pleasing her mother. But she did care about Rennie and what she thought of her. These last few weeks, a friendship had deepened between them, and a feeling of trust that was

46

new to Bess gave her a sense of security. At first, small confidences, which seemed to slip cautiously from Bess's mouth, found their way into the conversation as she and Rennie sat in front of the school or browsed around the shopping center. Gradually, as silently as the sun rose each morning and crept across her blankets, the bond between them had strengthened, and Bess was sure she could tell Rennie anything.

Rennie had encouraged her to try archery. Bess trusted Rennie's judgment and decided to test her talents at the sport.

The school gave archery lessons twice a week on the sprawling lawn behind the parking lot and tennis courts. Rennie had kept her promise to stay with Bess that first lesson, but now, as the targets stood in front of them, and the archers, many of them seasoned, lined in a row making their mark, Bess wondered if she and Rennie had made the right decision.

"They're all so good," Bess said, wincing.

"You'll be good, too," Rennie said, with such conviction that Bess felt it was already an established fact. Rennie had a way of saying things that sometimes seemed impossible, and making them exist by the sound of her voice or the look in her eyes.

Bess grew edgy as one archer after another, standing like a proud bowman, head straight, with barely a movement, filled the air with arrows, and only the far-off sound of the arrows hitting the targets broke the silence.

"Well," Rennie said at last, "the novices are going to start. That's you, kiddo."

Bess shook her head. "Don't remind me." Suddenly she hated her favorite cousin for getting married. He had started the whole thing. She pulled down her sweatshirt, which only added bulk to her figure. "Wish me luck," she said.

Rennie watched as her friend walked up to the novice line and an instructor came over. During the weeks that she had come to know Bess, Rennie had grown to understand what was behind the glib wise-cracks, the quick laughter, the jokes, the self-ribbing. She was such an honest person, with the kind of honesty that very few people understood or cared to know about.

Somehow Bess had let her know and understand. Perhaps it was because she hadn't encouraged Bess's jokes, hadn't found Bess, an unhappy Bess, very funny. "It's up to you," she had once told those serious blue eyes. "I mean, the weight thing. It could be the most important thing of every waking minute of your life, or you could decide once and for all what you really want to be, and then maybe your weight will be the least important thing of all."

She remembered Bess's answer. "Some Mondays when I get up, I want to be skinny and beautiful and have my body move like Puff, catlike, soft and grace-ful. But then on Tuesdays I don't care, and by Friday I'm eating more than ever."

Standing there, with the bow in her hand, Bess looked nervous and as uncertain about archery as she was about herself. Rennie bit her lip as her hands tightened on the arms of her wheelchair. She knew Bess so well now that she read her thoughts and some-times even suffered her indecisions. "What do I look like from the back? . . . Like a big wall." That's what Bess was thinking right now. Rennie ached for her friend's self-consciousness.

"Hi!" Lee touched the edge of the wheelchair, and Rennie looked up. Excitement stirred through her and roused memories of Mike and of yesterday's warm touches.

"Hi," she answered. She noticed the bow and arrow he carried. "Don't tell me."

"A regular Robin Hood." He sat down on the grass next to her.

"I'm fascinated." Rennie bent forward, watching

Bess learn how to hold the bow, how to look out of the sight. "Steady," the instructor cautioned.

A whistle blew. Someone motioned to Lee. "Be right back." He got up and ran over to the archers and took his place. Rennie watched him shoot. Arrow after arrow spun through the autumn air. His hands were so steady, so sure. Rennie had felt their strength when he had helped her up the stairs. She felt it now, and a chill went through her.

The hour passed very quickly. Rennie sat there, her attention alternating between Bess and Lee. Bess was clearly drooping. Her shoulders were hunched and, now and then, in between shots, she'd sit on the grass and stretch her arms as though she were putting them to sleep.

"Whoever told you it was easy, lied," Bess said, perspiring, as she came over to Rennie at the end of the session. "Why didn't someone tell me it was such work? I'm liable to lose weight out there." She threw her jacket over her shoulders. "I'm going to get a drink of water. Be right back." She lay the bow and arrow on Rennie's lap and ran into the school.

Lee ambled over to Rennie.

"I love it!" she exclaimed enthusiastically. "It's so beautiful, even just to sit and watch."

"Why just sit and watch?" Lee asked. "Want to shoot a few?"

The bow, warm in her hands, was tempting. Why not? "Sure," she answered, and wheeled over to the line. The grass was long and her wheelchair moved slowly. Now and then, Lee helped her push.

He put the bow in her hand, showing her how to hold it, his frame, behind the wheelchair, almost like an embrace. She leaned back and felt the hardness of his body against her head as he put the bow in her left hand and raised her right hand so it was close to her face. Through the sight on the bow, she saw the target in front of her, twenty-four yards away.

"You get six arrows at an end. That's at one time," he explained. "And there are four ends to a yardage. So you get twenty-four arrows. Think you can handle it? Remember to keep your arm motionless until the arrow hits."

He backed away from her, and the shelter was gone. The cool breeze hit her back. She knew he was standing off to the side, and she felt his eyes on her. She'd show him she could handle anything she made up her mind to handle!

She held the bow steadily and peered through the sight. There was a sudden stillness on the field. She noticed there were no other arrows piercing the air. The other archers were watching her. Robin Hood from a wheelchair. OK. If they wanted to watch, she'd give them something to watch.

She pulled the bow back and felt the string stretch. Then she let it go. Rennie heard the sound of wind as the string vibrated. The arrow went into the air and landed on the ground. It didn't even reach the target. She heard a low moan of disappointment run through the audience behind her. She looked back. Lee stood there leaning against a tree. "Go ahead," he encouraged her. "You've got twenty-three more arrows. Pull back farther. You didn't pull the bow back far enough."

She recalled her early years of basketball, preceding the wheelchair. The first time on the court, she had thrown the ball too hard. It had missed the basket. Quickly, she had learned to judge distance.

This is what she had to learn today—how to judge the distance. She could feel the target taunting her. "Laugh, clown, laugh," she jeered quietly back. Three, four, five arrows lost their way across the field.

And then one hit. Not a bull's-eye, but on the board! A stir broke the stillness behind her. An electricity shot through Rennie's hands. She shot another and another, excited by the challenge of the target that was filling up a little more.

When she was finished, her blonde hair was wet with perspiration, and she wiped it off her cheeks and off her shoulders as she rested back in the chair. She hadn't really participated in anything since she had been hurt except a few racing competitions. Sports had never been a big thing in her life before the accident. Yet today, here on the field, with the target still at the same range as for the able-bodied, she felt she had won an important victory, just as though the wheelchair hadn't been there at all.

Bess came over. "You don't need to lose weight. Stop showing me up." She wheeled Rennie off the field and onto the sidewalk.

"I like it, I really do," Rennie chattered excitedly. "I think I'm going to come here again. Come on, let's call my mother. She'll pick us up in front of the school."

"Hey, hold it!" Lee was running toward them. "Where are you two rushing off to?"

"Going to call my mother," Rennie said. She stopped pushing her wheelchair and looked back over her shoulder. "She's going to pick us up."

"Don't bother," Lee said as he caught up to them. "I'll drive you home. My car's over there." He didn't wait for an answer, just ran in front of them and unlocked the car door.

Bess looked at Rennie. Her eyes said all that was necessary. Rennie slid into the front seat, and Lee folded her wheelchair and put it in the back. Bess slid in, trying to squeeze into the space left by the chair.

From the back, where she was sitting, the two of them looked like any two people Bess had ever seen in a front seat. Rennie seemed to shed her wheelchair as easily as a heavy jacket on a cool spring day. With her long blonde hair spread across the back of the seat, watching her laugh and flirt as she looked up at Lee, it was difficult to remember that there was a chair at all.

Except that, at the moment, it was pushing against Bess's knee.

Lee and Rennie were deeply involved in their own conversation. Bess leaned back, content to have these moments to think about Josh, but that made her hungry. Thoughts of food and Josh seemed to run together. She dismissed both of them and thought of her birthday instead. Her mother had suggested that she have a party. She had considered it. Perhaps it would be nice to ask some of the girls, maybe Rennie and Elaine and Amy. Mentally, she made a note of a few more. Even as she did this, she couldn't wait to get to her mental list of boys. She looked toward the front seat. Lee . . . that would make Rennie happy. And, of course, Josh. A few more names were added to the list.

The wheelchair tires pressed against her legs, leaving black marks on the skin. Bess tried to change her position and moved closer toward the front seat. Meanwhile, the party was taking shape, with images of laughing faces filling her home, Josh's face, and Rennie and Lee and music and cake. She'd do it. She'd have the party . . . and she'd lose weight, not for the wedding, not for her mother, but for her own birthday. She'd lose weight for herself.

"Hey," she said from the back seat, "I'm going to have a party."

Rennie turned around, her eyes bright with excitement. "For what?"

"My birthday party."

Lee pulled up in front of Bess's house. "I can't get out," Bess said, grunting. "I'm packed in here for life."

Lee went out and opened the back door. Bess put out her arm, and Lee pulled as she dislodged herself from the back seat.

He laughed. "Do you see what you can do with some determination?"

"I meant it," she said, leaning into his opened

window. Bess looked over at Rennie who was sitting a little closer to Lee now. "Will you both come to my birthday party?" If they said yes, it would be easier to ask Elaine and Al and Amy and . . . Josh. Perhaps then she would get up the nerve to ask him.*

Lee hesitated. "It depends on the night," he said. "You know I work in the tie shop two nights a week."

"What about a Saturday night?"

"Till nine," he answered.

"OK. I'll start the party about nine. How about it?"

"Sounds fine to me," Rennie said, smiling. She was trying to act nonchalant, but her heart was pounding out of her chest. Her first party. It would be her first party since . . .

"Look, let us know the date." Lee started the car. He left Bess standing there with a triumphant smile on her lips.

Rennie watched through the rear-view mirror as her friend faded out of sight. Lee pulled into her driveway. He made no move to get out, but just stretched his arms and his long legs, which seemed to disappear somewhere under the dashboard.

"I really appreciate your driving me home," Rennie said. "You know, I think I'd like to try archery again."

"Twice a week, Monday and Thursday." There was a moment of comfortable silence. "Look," he said, "I'll be glad to drive you home after archery. There's no sense in your mother coming over, when I'm there with the car anyway."

"Well, if you'd like to sometimes, that would be great. My mom drives me so many places," she confided to him. "Sometimes I wish that she had more of a life of her own.'

"I know what you mean." Lee turned serious. "Since my father died, it's been tough for my mother. Work and me. Sometimes I feel it gets to be a heavy load for her. You know what I mean, sometimes I just feel sorry that I'm part of that load."

"That's just how I feel." Rennie looked at him, surprised that they felt so much alike. "With the wheelchair and everything, there are so many times when I feel my mother would be much happier if she just had herself to worry about." Lee looked at her thoughtfully. It was unusual to meet a girl of her age who was so direct, so honest about her feelings. For a moment he was silent, yet there was no awkwardness between them in the car. "You know," he said as he played absentmindedly with strands of her long blonde hair that had somehow fallen into his hand which now rested on her shoulder, "last week I was watching a telethon. There was a little girl on the program. She came with her mother, but the kid was on braces—you know, walking. Rennie, do you ever use braces?" He twirled her hair, and the softness of it over his hands seemed to sweep over his body as well.

The question caught Rennie unprepared. She drew in her breath, remembering the clinic and the braces in the closet. It was as if he had unlocked a secret door, a door that no one else would dare open, and now he was stepping inside. She was frightened, and her heart began to pound. "Don't come in," she wanted to say. "Don't try or you'll be like all the rest." But instead she just said, "No," softly. "It's easier for me in the wheelchair."

She didn't tell him about the braces in the closet, nor about how sore they made her body. She didn't tell him that when she wore those pieces of iron that went halfway up her body, she felt like a wobbly puppet. She did not mention the sores under her armpits from the crutches, nor the feeling of being a stick standing in the wind. If those words were somewhere in her eyes, he didn't see them.

"You don't seem the type to take the easy way out." He let his fingers drop from her hair. "If you could get on braces, heck, you could walk." He was thinking of her being lifted daily up the three steps, of being dependent on the wheelchair and on people's help. He didn't understand why she wouldn't want to walk if she could.

She grew quiet, only the stillness was different this time. It was the stillness of retreat, of refuge, and Lee caught a glimpse of Rennie's lips trembling as he spoke.

"Look," he said as he touched her hand, "I didn't mean to say anything to upset you." She looked up at him and, somewhere in her eyes, he felt there were answers he couldn't understand.

She smiled. "No problem," she said, and he knew it was all right again.

Lee took out the wheelchair and opened it up. Rennie slid into it from her side of the car.

"I'll pick you up for Bess's party, whenever it is." He stated it as though it were a fact they had both lived with for a long time.

Rennie sat there watching his car pull out of the driveway. Then, pushing the wheelchair against the fall leaves, she wheeled back to the maple tree at the side of the house, the tree whose leaves hung over the side carport and spread shade with what was left of their orange-yellow shelter.

Leaves, wide and heavy, slapped down upon the arms of her chair and glided lightly to the ground as Rennie sat there, feeling as though she were in a race, as though someone had thrown her into a big chariot and yelled, "Run the race, Rennie, run the race and win!"

Was this a real date, Bess's birthday party? Her first date with Lee.

She took out a piece of paper from her notebook and, while leaves playfully touched her head and fell about her shoulders, she began to write. *"Dear Carol, I'm in love. . . ."*

Bess's New Image

Bess stood naked in front of the mirror. She seemed to fill it with her flesh. A deep sigh passed through her body as she stood there for a long moment, letting the image of the mirror seep in. She put on her nightgown, then sat on the bed, with the window shade drawn up just enough to let the stars find their way in.

Puff jumped up on the bed and brushed against her arm as though she understood the importance of the night. Her fur, gray with flecks of orange and white, created the impression of the cat being fat, though when Bess picked her up and took her in her arms, she was light and soft to the touch. She let her face rest on the cat's fur and felt Puff's purring motor begin to hum.

"I love you, Puff . . . . I love you because you're the prettiest cat and because you listen to me, and because I know you love me." The cat closed her eyes in agreement and fell asleep in Bess's arms.

Bess sat there against the pillows, too determined to fall asleep. She had a plan of action, a definite plan of action. She would get up in the morning and not even enter the kitchen. She'd just skip breakfast. She was sure she could make it to lunch without fainting.

At lunch, she'd sit next to Rennie, as usual. Rennie would stop her from eating any junk. The after-school snack was the tough time of the day. Maybe she'd go over to Rennie's then and they could sweat it out together. Dinner with her mother and father would be no problem at all. She could always count on them to remind her not to take seconds. And she could go to bed early and miss the late snack. Her stomach growled at the thought of it. She patted it. "Don't worry," she comforted herself. "It'll all be worth it. It's for Josh."

Her mother came into the room, her long dressing gown smelling of something new on the market.

"Honey," she said, sitting on the bed, "Dad and I were talking tonight. We're looking into some diet camps for this summer. We'd like to make arrangements for you to go back to one of those camps again."

Bess shook her head. "Not me," she said. "What good did the camp do, anyway?"

"You did lose some weight, Bess. And really, this time it's getting out of hand."

"I gained it all back. And I hated the camp," Bess said angrily. "Besides, I've made up my mind to lose some weight in the next couple of weeks. You'll see a big change in me. I promise."

Bess's mother stood up with a sigh. "We've heard that one before, Bess. But those promises always found a way to be broken. We've made up our minds. Someone has to do something, and you, obviously, can't do it alone."

Bess's face grew hot. "Why don't you just leave me alone?"

"That's just the point. We can't. What would become of you if we did?" Her mother's remark had a sting of truth to it. For a moment, it hung like a sword between them. Bess sat there on the bed, her eyes closed, her arms tight around Puff, but feeling her mother's svelte figure in front of her. She just couldn't understand. If her mother gained a pound, she ate a little yogurt or cut out the bread and the big deal was over. How could she know what it felt like not to remember when the pounds blended into inches that circled your body and held it prisoner. Bess didn't remember when it all had begun, but now it wasn't just a pound or a bit of yogurt. At last the sweet perfume and the dressing gown left the bedroom.

Lying in bed that night, Bess thought about her party. It was better than thinking about diet camp. Some of her friends would bring her brightly wrapped gag gifts. She would be extra funny, and they would laugh and hold their stomachs and say, "Bess, you're a riot." Josh would be there sitting near the piano. His handsome face would spread into a grin, and he would clap his hands, shouting, "More . . . more."

She thought about the dress she would wear, the new one, the long one her mother had bought her. "It'll add height to you," she had said. It was dark green with a round neck. She'd pin her hair back and swoop it up. Her hair, long past her waist, swung across the pillows as she shifted her position. She could see it in the night, its reddish glow blending with Puff's fur.

She hadn't asked Josh yet. That was the thing. The others had said yes. She had made up her mind that tomorrow would be the day, but she had said that yesterday and the day before. Only time was running out, and she knew it had to be tomorrow.

"More, Bess, more." If Josh coaxed her, she'd sit at the piano and play just for him all night. She'd feel light, insignificantly light as her fingers would brush the keys and bring the room to life. And Josh would ask for more and more.

Everyone would come. She knew it. Didn't they all say, "Bess, we have such great times when you're around. Good ole Bess"? Bess turned into the pillows. Everyone knew her for years. She was as predictable, as familiar as the little statue in front of the park that kept getting wet from the lawn sprinkler. The water kept sprinkling all summer, every summer, and the statue stayed there and people would watch it glisten and drip. There was the man on the horse, dependable like Bess, or Mrs. Jensen's tulips, red and yellow, that began to grow each and every spring. Bess could count on the same colors growing in precise rows— and somehow, though they were pretty, the prettiest tulips on the block—the fact that they were so predictable somehow took away a bit of the excitement that their beauty promised.

Bess thought about that. Suddenly she sat up wide awake. Annoyed, Puff crept away and curled at the foot of the bed. Maybe that was her problem. Everyone could count on her to be the same, and she was. Even when she was at her best she must get boring because she didn't change. She touched her hair thoughtfully. Over and over again, she drew it across her shoulders and fingered the long ends. She wondered. All these years the long hair lay like a familiar rug on her back. It was part of Bess. Lately, it had seemed like an extra load, just something big stacked on something bigger. Hair shouldn't feel like a heavy rug to be carried around.

The shag. Rennie had come into school talking about her mother's new shag earlier that day. It was short, neat and sophisticated, Rennie had said, and her mother looked like a different person.

A smile replaced the sullen look, and Bess turned off the light, anxious for the morning. Tomorrow would be the day of change in her life. Tomorrow, without telling anyone, she would go over to the beauty shop after school, and that would be the beginning of the new Bess.

She fell asleep with Puff curled around her toes in a big circle of warmth. "Puff," she murmured sleepily, "tomorrow you'll be curling around the foot of the new me."

The next day she broke her promise to herself and told Rennie at archery about her plans. Rennie pulled back the bowstring and shot a bull's-eye. With Bess whispering over her head, it was difficult for Rennie to hold her hand steady but, with a determination that was now becoming her trademark, Rennie closed one eye, squinting against the sun, and released the string again.

Bess admired her, her drive to do whatever she did with everything she had. "What do you think? What do you think?" Bess kept pacing around the wheelchair trying to get Rennie's attention.

"Are you sure, Bess? You know, once it's cut, that's it." Rennie put down her bow and arrow and looked over at Bess's hair shining in the sunlight, "It's so pretty," she said wistfully. "And you can do so much with it long." Then she turned back to the target. "Why do you want to do it?" The arrow shot through the air and hit its mark.

Bess sat down on the grass next to her and put down her bow on her lap. There had been honesty between them right from the start. That had been the beauty of their relationship. Whatever was in Bess's heart or on her mind came out of her mouth without fear in any discussion with Rennie. There was no faking it. "I have to do something," she said seriously, "if I'm going to change myself."

Rennie looked down at her and stopped shooting. "You didn't ask Josh yet?"

Bess shook her head.

"You think cutting your hair will help?"

"It might," Bess said and shrugged. "It'll be a new me. Anyway, it's worth a try. I have to start somewhere."

Rennie wanted to tell her friend she could start with some will power and determination, but she thought better of it. She had no right to talk about such things. Just yesterday Lee had said again, "Why don't you try walking on the braces, Rennie?" She had pushed his words away, not wanting to face them. The physical therapist was still calling to find out how things were going, and Rennie was still ignoring the braces, now in the corner of her room. The parallel bars were up and waiting, yet nothing was happening. She couldn't offer advice to others. Not now.

"OK," she said at last. And then, looking at Bess's lost look, she smiled. "I'll go with you."

"Oh, great. I knew you would." Bess jumped up and started shooting again. If there was a target in front of Bess, she didn't see it. Her arrows, free, wild, with no controlling force behind them, flew joyously and without purpose into the air.

After archery, Rennie wheeled over to her. "Lee said he'd drive me home today. He can drop us off at the beauty shop."

"Good. It's only a couple of blocks from my house. Your mother can pick you up there later."

All the way to the beauty shop, though Rennie and Lee kept the conversation alive, Bess was conscious only of her cold hands and her hair. She didn't dare look at her hair. She didn't dare change her mind.

Lee dropped them off and looked quickly at his watch. "Have to get going," he said. "I'm supposed to relieve Mr. Dansick tonight."

He left them at the door of the beauty shop. Bess pushed, the door opened, and Rennie started to wheel in. The edge of her wheels hooked on to the side of the doors. "I can't quite make it," she said.

Bess looked at her stunned. None of them had even thought about the fact that the doorway entrance might be too skinny for Rennie's wheelchair.

Rennie edged her way back on the sidewalk. "Look," she said, "you go on in. I'll wait for you out here."

Bess's cheeks were red with anger, as she looked at the door and her friend Rennie, stuck on the outside. "You sure you won't mind?"

"Go ahead . . . I'm fine. I'll watch you from the window." Rennie wheeled over to the picture window at the front of the shop. "I'll be able to see everything," she said.

Rennie stayed there, watching Bess sit down in the chair and put the white towel around her shoulders. The beautician stood behind her covering her body with his tall silhouette. How could she have neglected to even wonder if the doorway was wide enough? Though she probably would have come anyway. But it was typical of her forgetfulness lately.

Something else was on her mind, constantly, in place of school, in place of everything that had been so constant in her life. Rennie stared into the big window as Bess's hair fell to the beauty parlor floor. A nagging worry lingered with her throughout the night. Although she had this standing date for Bess's party, though Lee and she had talked in the halls and he had driven her home, there had been no other dates. He never said, "How about a movie?" or, "Let's go bowling" or anything else. He would take her home and talk in the car about his father or his family or the future, wherever it was. Sometimes, he'd come in and talk with her mother or have a cup of coffee. But nothing else. He had never asked her out on a real date.

Rennie took out the letter she had received from Carol that morning and reread it.

I'm so afraid you're going to get hurt. Rennie, be careful. Lee is able-bodied. He's a walker, not a gimp. He's on the other side. Don't forget it. He can be nice to you and smile and drive you home, but when it comes down to the nitty gritty, he's still on the other side. People don't cross over.

They don't let you cross over, either. Believe me,
I know . . . .

Rennie shut her eyes for a moment, not wanting to
face the reality in the words in front of her. Lee was
different. She knew it. In her heart, she knew it. She
felt the wheelchair was becoming less visible to him.
He put it in the back of his car so quickly now, so
naturally, almost as though it were a valise. And she
could transfer and slide into the seat next to him so
casually. Without a ripple. He seemed hardly to notice.

But still, aside from school and home, they had been
in the shadows, their friendship blossoming without
any sun.

Rennie looked up. A red river of hair lay below
Bess. She watched the pool under Bess's chair grow
higher and higher, a red sea that was supposed to hold
all of the old Bess. Rennie wondered if it was possible to cut away the old part of you and leave it on
the hairdresser's floor. She hoped so. She hoped, for
Bess's sake, it could be so.

The hairdresser stepped away, and there was Bess,
staring at herself in the mirror. The beautician wheeled her around so that she could see all sides.

It had made a change. Even from the outside, Rennie could see the maturity that the long locks had hidden. A hint of glamour looked back at her through
the window.

Bess ran out the front door. "Do you like it? I do
look different, don't I? I do . . . I do!" She was jump-
ing up and down and talking at the same time, as she
circled Rennie's wheelchair excitedly, fluffing her hair,
touching it, flipping her new shag this way and that,
shaking her head and letting the curls enclose her face.

The long-haired youthfulness had left her. The shag
had made a difference. Rennie looked closer to see
what the new ingredient was. Confidence. She settled

on that word, because it seemed to fit just right. And Bess's face. It looked slimmer, and pretty, coming out into its own as though for the first time.

"Does your mother know?" Rennie asked as they wheeled down the sidewalk. "You did tell her?" The thought hit Rennie suddenly, and she turned and looked up at Bess.

"No," Bess said proudly. "It was my own decision."

Rennie looked ahead, disappointed. It had all been a spite job. Perhaps Bess didn't even know it, but she had cut her hair without telling her mother to shock her, to have one up on her, and the old tug-of-war was still on. Maybe she had done the right thing, but now it seemed for all the wrong reasons.

Josh was raking the leaves in front of his lawn when they went by.

"Ask him now," Rennie whispered.

Bess smiled at Josh as he looked up. Yes, with Rennie there, it would be easier. More casual.

"Hi," Bess called.

Josh waved, gathered the leaves and put them in a pile. They formed a multicolored package of autumn.

"I'm having a party," she called over the rustle of leaves.

He walked over toward her. "What did you say?"

Bess hesitated. She wasn't sure she could say it twice. "I'm having a birthday party. Just a couple of kids. Thought you might like to drop over."

"When?"

"Next Saturday night. About nine."

"Sounds OK," he said, and a small breeze stirred the pile of leaves. "I'd better dump them," Josh said, beginning to gather them up, "before I have to rake them up again."

Just as they were about to cross the street, Josh called, "Hey, what did you do with your hair?"

Bess shrugged and threw up her hands and laughed.

"Well, I did it," Bess shouted jubilantly as they approached her house. "I did it and it's over and he said OK. You heard him. OK. How about coming in?"

Bess looked at the steps in front of her house.

Rennie shook her head. "You call my mother. If I was going to stay a while, it would be worth the hassle of getting up them."

"OK." Bess ran into the living room. She forgot all about her hair. She was just thinking of Josh and the way his hair and cheeks matched the fall leaves. She picked up the phone eagerly and dialed.

"Mrs. Jackson. Rennie's at my house. Could you come and pick her up?"

She had just put the phone down when her mother exploded behind her.

"What did you do to your hair?" Bess's mother stood in front of her, with her mouth open, surprise, then hurt filling her eyes.

"Do you like it?" Bess turned around, showing off the red curls that edged her neck. She felt almost giddy. Her mother had always told her what she should do about herself, how she could make herself look better. Now, finally, she had come to her own great decision concerning what was good for her. And it had worked out well.

"All that beautiful hair—gone." Her mother's voice faded into helplessness as she came closer to Bess, close enough to let her fingers run through the layers of shag. "Why in the world did you do it? Why didn't you ask me first?"

Bess didn't answer. She felt her mother hadn't liked anything about her for so long that it didn't seem to matter. One more thing on the liability side seemed more right than wrong.

"Why didn't you tell me?" Anger now was turning to a sound of loneliness.

"I have to go outside. Rennie's there."

"Rennie will wait. I asked you a question. Why

didn't you tell me?" Her mother's eyes seemed to look deep inside her own, searching for the answer.

"It wasn't important to you. It was my hair. It was important to me." She walked past her mother. "It's rude to let Rennie sit out there alone."

"I want to talk to you about it," her mother said softly, the gentleness only irritating Bess more.

Bess turned around, a rueful smile on her lips, a smile new to her face and unusual for the good nature that always was there in its place. "Talking about it won't do any good, will it?"

For a second they stood there, just looking at one another, a woman close to forty who seemed spilling over with questions, and a girl about to step into sixteen who wasn't about to answer any of them.

Bess's face was stormy when she went outside. She and Rennie sat in silence by the front steps, not knowing that at that moment Mr. Dansick was in the tie shop, on the floor, his heart fighting to keep alive. He was lying in a pool of blood.

The Shooting

Lee stood in the tie shop. A small red stain spotted the floor. He walked over to it, his hands in his pockets, a tightness traveling from his throat to the pit of his stomach. Nauseated, he turned away toward the policeman taking notes near the rack of cotton ties.

"You work here?" he asked Lee.

Lee nodded.

The policeman asked him his name. He tried to control his voice as he answered, "Lee Snyder." He watched the policeman as he walked around the tie shop, kneeling now and then to examine bits of material on the floor, making quiet comments to himself.

"When did it happen?" Lee's voice shook and he cleared his throat. His knees felt weak, and he leaned on the glass casing that enclosed the wallets and watches that Mr. Dansick had lined neatly in small rows.

"An hour ago. Two guys came in, emptied the cash register, and pumped a bullet into his stomach."

Lee saw the half-filled coffee cup on the counter. An hour ago would have been three o'clock. Mr. Dansick always drank his coffee at three. He ate his doughnut and dunked it in the coffee, waiting for Lee to come in.

It was a ritual. Mr. Dansick was full of rituals like that. The coffee cup was always empty at three-thirty. Standing on the counter half-filled, it was evidence of what happened that day.

Lee shook his head. He knew that behind him was the circle of blood marking the spot where Mr. Dansick had fallen. Yet part of his mind kept insisting that Mr. Dansick had just stepped out for a short walk around the block, or to taste a new sandwich at the luncheonette across the street. "How bad is he?" he asked.

"Not good. He's an old man. That's not in his favor. It's a shame it had to happen to him. He's been here such a long time." The policeman seemed to sum it up to his own satisfaction. He closed his notebook. "Yeah, I think someone said he's been here thirty years."

The neighborhood had been different thirty years ago. During those winter nights when they had worked together, Lee had listened to Mr. Dansick telling him how different everything had been. Mr. Dansick had built his tie shop right in the center of towering brick houses. Selling ties all those years to fathers and sons, he knew that blue went with this one's eyes, and green with someone else's suit, and stripes with another one's mod pants; he had offered advice throughout all the years while the buildings showed wear with passing of time. The customers had changed, too. Some were the same, but many others walked around with hard faces. They didn't smile back at Mr Dansick's jokes. Still he stayed. "You don't desert a family just because they face hard times," he said. "Why should I desert the neighborhood?"

Lee sat on the stool in the corner. Even now the neighborhood wasn't really bad. Maybe a little disenchanted with life and struggling to survive, but not hopeless. These weren't the type of people from whom you'd expect a bullet in the belly.

"They got in a car," he heard the policeman say. "Probably don't live around here. Someone thought they came from the Hanson section, across town."

Lee felt a relief at the possibility that they weren't any of the boys Mr. Dansick had watched grow up, or someone whom he had helped through hard times. Did it matter, though? With a bullet in his belly, would it matter to Mr. Dansick?

Lee looked up as a stir of excitement flooded the front door. Customers were coming in, confused, mixing with the police. One of the policemen ushered them out, closed the long windowed glass door and walked over to Lee.

"Well, son, I guess the shop will be closed up for a couple of weeks. You might as well go home. We'll call you if we have any more questions."

"What hospital is Mr. Dansick in?"

"Sacred Heart."

Lee looked back at the closed tie shop door just before he got into his car. "I never closed the doors during the week," Mr. Dansick had boasted. "In thirty years the doors have always been opened for business." Mr. Dansick hadn't counted on a piece of lead in his stomach.

Lee drove over to the hospital, exhaustion wiping away the energy that he could always count on to get him through the day. His stomach still felt twisted inside. He loved Mr. Dansick and he loved the tie shop. For the past two years, he had felt at home there. Through all the plans for college and the future his mother dreamed about for him, he couldn't imagine feeling more purposeful than when he was unpacking the ties, or setting them in rows, or greeting the familiar faces he had come to know. "Family," Mr. Dansick reminded him, "they're all family. Mr. Bilkins likes bright ties. Show him that long one, down to the waist. It'll give him a laugh." And then, "Mr. Jenkins, why no smile today? Come in. Our ties will make you happy." A laugh. A handshake. A reaching out. Mr. Dansick knew who carried troubles on his shoulders, where illness affected a family. Sometimes he seemed like a great diagnostician, searching people's eyes and coming up with the right response.

"I love my customers." He'd smile, and his white hair would fall down over his forehead in agreement. "People don't care about their customers today," he'd say, unpacking his dinner and putting it on the hot plate. The old man's voice kept coming back to Lee during his ride to the hospital. A widower for five years, Mr. Dansick had grown accustomed to eating at the store. "Other places, they treat people like a number. Not here. Here, people are fathers and sons, daughters picking out gifts, mothers afraid the tie might be wrong for the husband."

Somewhere between Mr. Dansick's philosophy of life and his rituals, the job had become something more significant to Lee than just reporting to work. It had seemed a way of life. Simple, uncomplicated. A direct route to other human beings. Stacking those ties and unpacking those boxes seemed as necessary as planting a crop or tilling the soil. There were moments when he thought he knew how farmers must feel, perhaps even how pioneers must have grown possessive of their land. Though it wasn't his shop, Lee had shared the enthusiasm of one man believing in what he did.

Lee parked in the hospital lot, then looked up at the windows, tiny lights piled up on top of one another. Surely Mr. Dansick was alive. He had to be. Lee ran up the front steps. He hadn't, until this moment, even considered the fact that Mr. Dansick might die. He could have died in the ambulance, or could be dying right now, as Lee ran into the lobby.

He stopped at the front desk, out of breath. "Mr. Dansick. Could I see him?"

The nurse looked at the list in front of her. "Are you a relative?"

"No."

"Well, I'm sorry. No visitors allowed."

"But he doesn't have any relatives here. They're in California."

She picked up the phone. "What's your name?"

"Lee Snyder."

He leaned against the side of the wall, feeling a weakness creep about his knees as he waited. Why was it taking her so long? She spoke to someone on the other end of the phone and then looked up.

"Third floor. He's in the hallway, ready for surgery."

"Can I go up?"

"Yes. He's been asking for you."

Lee ran up the steps to the third floor without waiting for the elevator.

White suits, nurses' uniforms, caps and pretty faces weaved in front of him, and then he saw a stretcher by a desk. White, almost as white as the sheets, Mr. Dansick lay there, his eyes closed, his face showing pain.

Lee stood there, unable to speak. There were tubes, like small antennae, sticking out from Mr. Dansick's arms and from somewhere under the sheets. His lips were parted and strangely blue. Lee felt the presence of death somewhere in the room.

A doctor came over. "We've just taken X rays. We're going to take him up to see what damage the bullet has done. Are you his son?"

He looked down at Mr. Dansick. He had stepped into his life just when Lee's father had died. "Be a good boy, Lee. Take care of your mother. Hard work, honesty, don't lie to yourself." Which words were Mr. Dansick's? Which his father's? Somewhere blended in with the ties were a father and son working together. He shook his head. "I work for him," he said hoarsely. He straightened the wrinkled sheet which lay over Mr. Dansick's body. "But he's like my father," he added quickly, afraid the doctor might send him away. And then, "Can he speak? Is he conscious?"

"Now and then."

Mr. Dansick's eyes opened. A pasty smile crossed his lips, and they seemed to crack from the strain. "I thought I heard your voice," he said. He tried to lift his arm, but the tubes held him back.

"Hey, don't move." Lee bent down beside him.

"Thirty years," Mr. Dansick murmured. "Never closed." His eyes shut, then they opened again with a brightness that startled Lee. "Lee, keep the shop open. You can manage. Call Harry. He'll work in the day-time. You come in nights." He closed his eyes, then smiled again. "They think a bullet can stop Dansick." His voice grew weaker. "It's a war between bullets and people." The blue eyes clicked on again. "Call Harry," he said roughly. "Don't let me down, Lee. Keep the shop open."

The doctor stood listening. Mr. Dansick was re-peating the instructions over and over as though he had put the message on a recording. "Tell him you'll do it," the doctor advised softly. "We've got to give him something to go into the operating room with."

"OK." Lee bent down closer so that he was nearly touching Mr. Dansick's cheek. "I'll take care of everything. Don't worry, Mr. Dansick. The shop won't close."

"You might as well leave now," the doctor said, starting to move the stretcher. "He'll be upstairs for a couple of hours. Come back later. Maybe then we'll have something good to tell you."

The shop won't close. Lee had said it as though he owned it, as though the shop had been his from the start. Why did he make promises which he might not be able to keep?

Lee left the hospital. The day had begun so simply. If only he could spin the clock back to the morning and stop there. He sat behind the wheel in the parking lot, not certain for a few moments where he wanted to take the car. He didn't want to go home. Not now. His mother, with her plans for college, for Michigan and everything she was working for, didn't fit into the picture tonight. He couldn't tell her about his promise to Mr. Dansick. As it was she felt his work at the tie shop was interfering with his studies now. She wouldn't be happy to hear that he would have to spend even more time on this job, which she considered temporary and unimportant for his future.

But he wouldn't be able to keep it from her. Where could he hide his own happiness at being able to keep the tie shop open? Tonight when Mr. Dansick had put the future of the shop, and the challenge of keeping it alive, in his hands, Lee had felt an exhilaration that would be difficult to explain to his mother or to anyone else. He remembered Billy Bean. "Hey, Lee, I'll be back Tuesday. Have a sharp date that night. Find a tie for this shirt." He had left the shirt on the counter.

Billy Bean and the others. "Mr. Dansick should retire," his mother had said so many times. She would never be able to understand either him or Mr. Dansick.

Lee drove down the city streets, eliminating destinations one after the other. He thought of Jo and how easily she could make him forget Mr. Dansick, and probably everything else, except her warm hands. But he didn't want to forget. He wanted to go somewhere where he could share what he wanted to remember, what he knew he must do. He found himself in front of Rennie's house. He looked at his watch: eleven o'clock. He had been oblivious of time ever since he saw that stain on the floor. The hours seemed to rush by. He remembered his father's death and the funeral. First he was on the floor in the bathroom, then in the casket, then in the ground. Almost an out-of-breath procession that slid by so quickly that he wanted to stop the burial, stop the machine that would take his father out of sight forever. Then he was gone, and people were back at their house eating, while Lee had wondered why everyone got hungry at funerals. He had watched the food disappear and heard the hushed, then louder conversation that seemed to grow more animated as the hours went by. All the while, he sat there not believing that the room upstairs, with a man's clothes still hanging in the closet, was without his father. The following week he had decided to get a job, and Mr. Dansick's big sign in the window, "Come in, if you like hard work and can be on time," had appealed to him. At least the guy was honest.

Lee watched the lights flick off in the living room of Rennie's house, then in the kitchen. He stood outside his car, wanting to stop the first floor of the house from darkening, but then he saw the top lights in the bedrooms shine across the curtains and his heart sank. He couldn't bring them all downstairs again.

A face peered from the upstairs window. The window opened. "Lee, is that you out there?" Mrs. Jackson called out softly.

For a moment, he felt foolish being caught standing there on the front lawn. But the feeling passed. He needed to talk to someone. He wanted to talk to Rennie.

"I know it's late," he said. "Is Rennie sleeping?"

Mrs. Jackson left the window for a moment, then came back. "I'll be right down."

Lee apologized when the front door finally opened, but Mrs. Jackson smiled. "If you stop over at this time of night, there must be a good reason."

Lee knew that somewhere around the corner, Rennie was bouncing down the steps from the bedroom. He tried not to think about it. It disturbed him, and the fact that it did made him uneasy.

"Hi." Rennie wheeled into the living room. She was wearing a green bathrobe that turned her eyes a shade greener.

"Rennie, turn out the lights when you go to bed." They heard her mother's voice as she was making her way upstairs. A door shut somewhere at the top of the house, and they were alone.

"What's wrong?" She saw it in his eyes and she helped him by asking.

"Mr. Dansick got shot tonight."

The impact of his words brought pain to her eyes, those green eyes that moments before had seemed lit up with excitement.

"Not Mr. Dansick." She swallowed hard as though fresh words were caught in her throat. "Why?"

"Robbery, the police think. They don't know who did it. They're operating on him now."

"Oh, my!" He watched those green patches disappear, as her eyes closed. "He's not going to die, is he?" she whispered.

Lee didn't answer. He sat down on the couch next to the wheelchair and took her hand in his, because holding it made him feel safer, a little more sure that Mr. Dansick wouldn't die. Her hand was strong, but soft and warm. It clung to his hand so naturally.

"It's a good neighborhood," he said, wondering whether he was trying to convince Rennie or himself. "It's not fair that a man's work should go down the drain. I was standing there, looking at his cup of coffee on the counter, and thought there should be more of Mr. Dansick left than that coffee. He gave more of himself to everyone. He has to leave more. Do you know what I mean?"

She closed her hand around his as her answer.

"He wants the tie shop to stay open. That's all he kept asking me to do. The doctor told me to promise him anything, to give him hope. But I don't want it to be just an empty promise."

"Can you help him do that? If it's so important to him, and to you? It is important to you, too, Lee, isn't it?"

He smiled, but a sad line crossed his face. A lot of people would think that funny, a little tie shop being important. Yet he wasn't embarrassed to admit to her that she was right.

Suddenly anger, like a quick storm, wiped the softness from Rennie's face. "If it's a man's life, it's important. It's important that a man's world shouldn't be stopped with a bullet and that no one should be able to walk in and wipe out his dreams."

Lee felt the anger in her fingers as they tightened on his hand. "No one has the right to say what is important for another human being and what isn't," she said, speaking for Mr. Dansick and for herself. The words slipped out, almost like a glass of milk tipping across the kitchen table.

Her remark caught them both by surprise. It was filled with such intense anger.

"Look," he said, "it's late. I've kept you up long enough. I want to get back to the hospital and see how he is."

"What are you going to do?" She looked up at him. He stood up, his hands in his pockets, and for a long moment he looked into the eyes that were asking him for an answer. He saw it there, in the smile that crept across her face, in the wordlessness that bound them closer together than he had ever been with a human being before. The answer was there in the room. He had brought it in with him, and she understood.

Lee drove back to the hospital. Two hours had passed. The woman at the desk said, "Nothing yet." Lee sat in the waiting room, wondering whether he should have asked Mr. Dansick earlier if there was anyone he wanted him to call, a sister or brother, instead of talking about the shop.

The doctor stood in front of him, the same doctor who had heard him make the promise to Mr. Dansick, upstairs. He sat down beside Lee on the black stiff couch. "Well," he sighed wearily, "he made it. There's a lot of damage in there. The bullet mixed up things pretty badly. But he's alive. And he's fighting. And he's not the type of man to lose."

Lee felt the rubber band inside his stomach snap in relief.

"He won't be himself for a long time," the doctor went on.

"He has a sister in California," Lee said, suddenly remembering.

"I'll get her name as soon as he wakes up. He's an old man, Lee, and a sick one, but he's got a good chance. He needs rest and care and peace of mind about that tie shop. It was on his mind right up to the time of his operation."

Lee left the hospital exhausted. Mr. Dansick had done his part. He had fought and survived the operation, and he was still fighting to get back on his feet. Now the rest was up to him. He would go back and open the shop, and he would take care of it until Mr. Dansick could return. And if it ran into months, he knew there would be no room in his life for Michigan State.

Tomorrow he would call Harry. Tomorrow he would make the necessary arrangements and break the news to his mother. But tonight, as he finally crept into bed and felt his body sink achingly into the sheets, he wanted only the luxury of one thought. As his eyes closed he thought of Rennie. Only she was not sitting in the wheelchair at all. She was walking.

Rejection

Rennie wheeled around the room excitedly, "Mother, hurry," she called, spreading first one dress on the bed and then another.

Mrs. Jackson ran in. "I found the skirt. I knew I had brought it back from the cleaners." She put the skirt on the bed. It was long and flowered, with velvet stretching to Rennie's feet. She pulled out a blouse from the closet and placed it in front of her.

"What do you think?"

"It's perfect."

Rennie put the skirt on her lap. She stayed away from long clothes as much as possible because of the wheelchair, but tonight was different. Tonight was Bess's party.

She saw the excitement in her mother's face and looked away. Tonight they both found it difficult to look at one another. Rennie was going out on a Saturday night, just like all the other girls in school.

"You have an hour yet." Mrs. Jackson ran the tub.

"I know, I know." Rennie didn't want to be late, not by a minute. One of the things she had learned during these months in a wheelchair was that getting ready for an appointment would take her hours longer than someone who walked. Planning ahead was important, and she had learned to lay out her clothes the night before school, to know where her books, pencils and homework assignments were, and know how long it would take her to take a bath and put on her makeup. She had it all down to a science.

Once in the tub, Rennie lay back and relaxed. It was OK. It would be all right. A night with Lee, at a party with music and laughter. She closed her eyes, and the picture of the two of them together focused in as sharp, as clear as ever. She tried to envision them in a special place. Yes, the couch, the big blue couch in Bess's living room. She would make sure they sat on a couch together. Lee had warned her already that they would probably get to Bess's party late. He was managing the tie shop for Mr. Dansick, who was still in the hospital. It meant working long hours after school, and he had to drop out of archery. And on Saturday night, the store closed at nine. But she didn't mind. She didn't see him as much in school lately, and that bothered her. And when they met to talk, his eyes seemed tired.

Tonight, for the first time, he called just to talk. "I'm really happy at the shop," he told her. "But I have the feeling it might develop into a full-time job."

Rennie lay in the bathtub with the lather soft about her body and the suds creeping around her arms and up under her chin. She had sensed Lee's inner tug-of-war during their conversation. His life was going in new directions. Would his mother approve of the changes?

"You know," he had said just before he hung up, "things could look pretty good for me right here in this town."

What things? She had wanted to ask. Among the things, does my being in this town make you want to stay on?

Rennie scrubbed her arms till they tingled. She

couldn't blame Lee's mother for having dreams, for wanting those dreams about Lee to come true. She was thinking of her own mother, still coaxing her to wear the braces. Her advice to Lee had been, "I guess, somewhere, your parents' dreams must end, and your own begin."

She had wanted to tell him about her own dreams tonight, but she kept them to herself. The moments that they had had together, though few, brought touches and looks that were new to both of them. She felt that. Once he motioned toward her face with his hand, as though he was going to touch her cheek, and he then pulled away.

Though that special moment had passed, she had felt it. And he had, too. It would come back. She believed that as strongly as she believed that braces weren't the answer in her life. Quickly, she checked the clock on the clothes hamper, then slid out of the tub and into the wheelchair.

When she finished dressing, Rennie looked into the mirror. With her blonde hair combed straight, just to her shoulders, and the makeup accenting her green eyes, she was pleased with her reflection in the mirror.

She wheeled into the living room just as the doorbell rang. Her mother answered the door, and Lee stood in the doorway. He looked at Rennie. Softly, as though the power was taken out of his voice, he said, "You look beautiful, Rennie," and then a flush crept up his neck. He cleared his throat, and Rennie knew he was ready to go.

"Better wear your winter coat tonight, Rennie," her mother suggested. "I think we've seen the end of fall." She put the coat around Rennie's shoulders.

"I'm sorry I'm late," Lee said as they got into the car. "I had trouble locking the door to the shop. We've changed all the locks since the robbery, and you have to have just the right touch with the keys."

Rennie tried to listen to what Lee was saying.

Usually his words were enough to push everything else out of her mind. But tonight was different. Her heart pounded underneath the green blouse, and her hands, cold and clammy, lay in her lap. What am I so nervous about? She asked herself over and over. It was the same Lee whom she saw at school, the same Lee who had driven her home from archery. She wasn't frightened then. Why now? She looked at Lee with his jacket and tie and a Saturday-night manner about him. She felt as though they were meeting for the first time, as though life had put them down in an entirely new setting. She wasn't as certain about herself in this new environment.

They were driving just a short time when Lee stopped the car and turned it around. "Boy, am I disorganized today." Rennie saw the same houses they had just passed parading before them again.

"Where are you going?"

"Back to my house. I forgot the gift for Bess. My mother bought her something, and I must have left it on the desk."

They pulled up in front of a yellow-and-black split-level house. It was a warm-looking home. A redwood fence lined the driveway, and brightly colored shutters decorated the windows. There were trees in front of the windows, and tall bushes almost covering the glass secluded the house from the street and gave it a look of privacy. Lee got out, then went around to Rennie's side of the car.

"I'll wait here," she said. "It's really too much bother." But he shook his head. "No, it isn't. Come on. I've been telling my mother all about you. It's time you two met."

Rennie hadn't counted on this. Whatever little poise she had been able to maintain deserted her now, and her hands grew moist.

Mrs. Snyder opened the door, holding Bess's present. When she saw Rennie, she opened the door wider. "Come in, please. Lee, I knew the moment I saw your car that you had forgotten Bess's gift."

"Mom, this is Rennie."

"Hello." She smiled, looking down at Rennie. "Lee has told me so much about you. You're really tops on his list."

Rennie blushed. She could feel Mrs. Snyder's eyes appraising her, examining her clothes and her hair. Her eyes went from Rennie to Lee, who stood behind the chair with an apparent look of pride.

"Mom, we just stopped in for a second. We really have to get going."

"Of course." Mrs. Snyder smiled again, this time an uncertain awareness clouding her eyes as she looked at Rennie again. Faint words that Rennie wanted to blot out came back to her, haunting her, taking stabs at her happiness. Carol's words: "Just don't get out of line, Rennie. Stay where you belong."

Once back in the car, she felt better. She looked at Lee. If she had any doubts, they were wiped away by the contentment that showed in his smile, the smile she had come to love, to depend on, to need.

They pulled up at Bess's house. All the lights were on and cars lined the driveway. Lee turned her wheelchair around so that he was in back of it and lifted it up the steps.

Amy opened the door. "Come on in," she said. Bess was sitting at the piano singing, and one of the boys from school sat on the floor near her, accompanying her with his guitar. The room was filled with familiar faces. Rennie wheeled around the room, greeting everyone. Bess's party was a success. The living room vibrated with conversation and music as some chose to dance and others to eat. Bess left the piano, and Rennie followed her into the kitchen. "Oh, Bess," she said excitedly, "the party's just great!"

Bess turned around. Her eyes were brimming with tears. "Is it? Is it really? Maybe for you," she said, running to the kitchen sink where she grabbed a dish towel and wiped her wet cheeks.

Suddenly Rennie knew what she was crying about. In her excitement she hadn't noticed nor even thought of Josh until now. He wasn't here.

"He didn't come," Bess said. "He didn't even call. You heard him. You were with me when I asked him. He said yes. But he didn't mean it."

Rennie touched her friend's hand and held it. "Come on, Bess. It's still early. Maybe he's working. He'll just come late, you wait and see."

"I don't think so. But maybe." Bess wanted to believe it. They returned to the living room, but Bess didn't play the piano or sing again that night. Her eyes clung to the front door, waiting. When her mother brought in a big cake with candles that lit up the room, Bess looked over at Rennie and they both knew Josh would not show up that night. They sang "Happy Birthday" while Bess opened up her presents. Rennie sat with Lee on the couch.

"I can't bear to look at her face," Rennie told him.

"I know. It was a raw deal. He could have called."

"I wish the party were over already. Everyone else is having such a great time it might never end."

Lee smiled. "I feel sorry for Bess, but I'm having a great time, too." he said. "And I wish it would never end."

Rennie rested her head against his shoulder. Forgive me, Bess, she thought, but this is the most beautiful evening of my life.

When the cake was served, Bess cut herself the biggest piece and ate two portions with a scoop of ice cream on each. Then, as though food were the weapon and she the one being punished, she made herself a platter and busied herself finishing up the leftover potato chips. Rennie winced as she watched her. Tonight, in her new dress, the pounds clearly diminishing, Bess had never looked better. She had spent these weeks before the party as disciplined as an athlete training for a game. Now she sat there at the buffet table recklessly throwing it all away—including the wedding in Washington.

During the evening someone asked, "Wasn't Josh supposed to be here?"

Before Bess could answer, a voice from the corner replied, "I thought he went skiing for the weekend."

Rennie put down her glass of soda on the table in front of them. Everyone else in the room was dancing. "Please ask Bess," she said to Lee.

He looked at her and hesitated. "I really don't dance well."

"Please," she insisted.

Lee shrugged and walked over to Bess. Soon they were on the floor, and Rennie realized that if Lee had never lied to her before, he had lied to her now. He danced beautifully, his graceful body making all the right moves, his feet feeling the rhythm without effort. Rennie felt herself slide down, inside, where the pit of her stomach was, inside where all the happiness had been only moments before. She grew angry at herself. What did she expect? That he would have two left feet? Did she want it that way because she would never be able to dance with him? Dancing hadn't seemed important before. But now, with the low lights and the music so soft, watching Bess in his arms, Rennie could only say to herself over and over, never, we'll never dance together.

When he came back, she was silent. If he read her thoughts, which lately he seemed to be able to do, he didn't let her know. "I think we'd better shove off," he said. "It's been a long night for Bess, and no one seems to be thinking of leaving. Let's start the ball rolling."

Rennie nodded in agreement. Lee opened her wheelchair and she slid into it. "Bess, it was a beautiful party," she said as they said their good-byes at the door. Bess was holding another piece of cake on her plate.

"I'm glad you enjoyed it, Rennie. I really am." Again the brown eyes clouded. She scooped up Puff with one hand and nestled her against her cheek. "What would I do without Puff?" Bess said and laughed. "She understands all my troubles."

"I do, too." Rennie said softly. "I'll see you in school Monday."

Rennie saw the sign for Eagle's Peak as they drove home. "I've never been there," she said.

"Where?" Lee asked. But he knew what she meant, and that she knew it.

"Eagle's Peak. I hear it's so beautiful, high up on the hill." She knew what she was saying and held her breath. She had never been so forward, not since the accident. Before that night Rennie would not have said it.

Lee hesitated. Then he turned and looked at her seriously. "I think you're trying to seduce me," he said. His face changed into a smile.

She laughed nervously, and he drove the car toward Eagle's Peak. Other cars stretched across the hill. They found a space and parked. She sat forward and looked out through the window, her arms leaning on the dashboard. "Isn't it something? The whole city spread out before us."

"You're something," Lee said, looking at her.

"I'm just a girl." That's all she wanted to be. An ordinary, average, nothing-special girl.

Lee shook his head. "I've never met anybody like you, Rennie. You've got so much courage." He started to say more, but she covered his lips with her fingers.

"Shh," she said. "Don't tell me about courage. I'm not a soldier. I'm just a girl, in school." She would have liked to add "and in love," but her good sense stopped her.

For a moment her fingers stayed on his lips and

traced them. She wasn't sure if she moved closer or if he gently pulled her closer, but she was in his arms and, for a brief moment, she felt his lips touch her hair.

Then, almost roughly, he pushed her back to her side of the car. He seemed flustered as he started the car. "It's time we went back," he said firmly. "I really have a lot of work to catch up with this weekend."

"I won't break. You know, I'm not made of spun glass." Could she tell him that? Was it fear that she was someone different? Once Carol had told her, "Some people think we're freaks." She looked over at him, her body trembling. Did he stop because he felt that? No, not him. But why? Was he afraid to kiss her? Would he have stopped with someone else? Did he stop with Jo, that girl from the ice cream shop, the one who stopped over at archery sometimes and tugged at his elbow when she walked by his side?

They drove home in silence. As he pulled the wheelchair out of the car, he said quietly, "You know, Rennie, I really wish you would give those braces a try. You went through so much to get them fitted. It would be great to see you standing."

She looked up at him. She would be about his height, perhaps a little shorter. He didn't even know how tall she was.

That night in bed she made up her mind. If Lee wanted her to stand, she would. She didn't want to ask herself why it was so important to him. She wouldn't ask herself any questions now that might break apart her happiness, her love.

With just the small bedlight on, she wrote to Carol.
Dear Carol,

I'm going to do it. Maybe Mom's right. And now Lee, too. I'm going to get on those braces and use them. I'm really going to try. Maybe this time it'll work. It could have been too soon at the Rehabilitation Center. Remember Sammy? He always wore braces. He hated the wheelchair. And Lila. She used to swing up the steps, easy as anything.

Lee wants me to try. It's important to him. I'd just about do anything he asked. I guess that's what love is all about.

Rennie

Conflicts

Life was getting complicated, Lee thought as he drove down the familiar street to the hospital. How had it all become one big maze, when only a couple of months ago it had all been so simple? Life's sudden jolts had taken the whole checkerboard he called living and dumped the checkers all over the place. Once he had been mowing lawns. Once he had been thinking about Michigan. Once he had been making love to Jo.

He was still making love to Jo, only it wasn't good because he was thinking of Rennie. And he talked to his mother about Michigan when he had no intention of going. And Mr. Dansick's tie shop was becoming more and more important in his life. But what was becoming more important than anything else now was Rennie. When he thought about her, something good happened inside him. He didn't want to think about her, and he tried to control himself many times because life seemed to spin around even more crazily when she was in his thoughts.

He'd look for her in the hallways. When he caught a glimpse of the chair, he felt drawn to her. Sometimes he ran right over. Sometimes he walked away, pretending not to see her. He didn't know why.

Rennie, with that smile and those green eyes and some inner drive that was fighting all the time to make it, gave him that special confidence to believe in her and in himself. There wasn't a girl in that school who could match her. She was young, but young with a maturity that grew out of her shocking accident. He looked to her for wisdom and for an unpredictable daring that surprised him constantly.

Lately, he was walking around like an idiot. Lee relaxed behind the wheel of the car, glad to be alone with his thoughts. Maybe if he shook them all out, like cleaning a closet, he'd be able to sort out the ones he wanted to keep. He knew he was running away from Rennie, and running the opposite way from Rennie seemed to be about the most unreasonable thing he had ever done in his life. She was the only one who understood about the tie shop and why his future in the shop seemed right for him. He could tell her of the challenge he felt in just operating a store that reached out to people. Alone here in the car he could be honest with himself. He winced as the truth forced its way out of his confused thoughts. He knew why he was running away from Rennie. It was because of his mother. At last the truth was out!

They had been so close all these years past. Then, suddenly, in the last few months, their words were strained, their smiles limited, the silent moments between them tight and uneasy. When they were alone, they had nothing right to say to each other. He'd come home from the tie shop, tired, unable to share his thoughts with her. His mother would say, "What a waste. You can't spend the rest of your life there." He'd see college and Michigan in her eyes. He couldn't blame her. But he knew Michigan was just the smoke screen. Eventually, each evening, they would get down to the heart of the problem.

"She's very pretty," his mother had said the night when he had returned from Bess's birthday party. "I didn't expect her to be so pretty. I mean, crippled and everything."

He hadn't asked and still didn't know what the everything meant.

Driving through the night, he tried to put the conversation back into place, like little pieces from a jigsaw puzzle. "It was really nice of you to take her, Lee. I guess she doesn't get out often."

It had angered him then, and the words lingered to anger him now. "Nice of me," he had said. "I took her out because I wanted to." He hadn't meant to say that. In fact, he hadn't realized that he had felt that way.

Only this morning, as he was leaving for school, his mother had closed the front door with the words, "I don't understand. With all those pretty girls at school, especially Jo, surely you're not serious about this crippled girl?"

His shout, "Stop calling her crippled," had landed like a slap upon his mother's face, and she had turned away, crying.

It was an ugly scene but one that had been played and replayed during the months he had been seeing Rennie. His mother's tears this morning had been the first tears he had seen since his father's death, and they cut into Lee like many tiny knives leaving their marks. He felt their scars even now, hours later.

"It's a pity, Lee, a real pity!" She had flung the words at him many times during the nights they tried to avoid the conflict by watching television or reading. But it hadn't worked. Somehow the words couldn't be stilled, and they edged their way past any attempts at peace.

Tonight, for the first time, he had lied to his mother. Her face was so pale, her eyes so tired. If he couldn't make her understand what was important in his life, he'd tell her what she wanted to hear. He told her that he hadn't made up his mind about school. That was a lie. But it was the second lie that had made his stomach curl, and even now it sickened him. He told her that he was just being nice to Rennie, that she was a very brave girl and that he was helping out her mother by driving her home. That was a lie, too.

His mother stopped crying. Her eyes had cleared almost immediately. He had become sick to his stomach, as though he had defiled Rennie. He wondered how he would be able to speak to Rennie again without feeling like a Judas.

Parking his car in the parking lot, Lee felt he would always remember tonight as the night he had quieted his mother's tears by renouncing Rennie.

He had promised. Promises were important to him. His mother knew that. He didn't make promises easily, nor did he ever break them. Now he was caught in a net of fake words that held him prisoner. He would try forgetting his treachery in Jo's arms. There, he hoped he would be safe from those green eyes that followed him to bed at night. He wondered why he felt threatened as he walked through the open door of the hospital. Who threatened him? Not Rennie, that so-called helpless girl called Rennie.

Perhaps he was just suffering from the jumpiness that high school graduation brought with it. The last year, and especially the last few months, were hectic, with plans and intentions that seemed vague and out of reach. His perspective, usually his greatest ally, had narrowed until now it seemed to work against him.

He took the elevator up to Mr. Dansick's room. He would put everything back in place again. He'd work at it, because life had been good before, comfortable and good.

"Hi, Mr. Dansick." Lee walked over to the bed. The small light in the room created an eerie cast. And the antiseptic smell, the type of windows, the stretcher-like beds and the pillows that always seemed puffed made Lee uncomfortable and suddenly anxious to leave.

Mr. Dansick sat up in bed. His face was gaunt and pale. He put up a thin hand to Lee's and held it.

"I'm glad you came," he said weakly. Then he patted the top sheet over his belly, saying, "Some bullet."

Lee nodded. "It's OK, though. The doctors say you're going to be great."

"I never was great before the shooting." Mr. Dansick smiled. "So how can I be great now?" He sighed. "Great, but not as good as new. My sister, she's coming from California tomorrow. I should be leaving the hospital sometime next week."

"Good. The tie shop is just fine." He answered the question he saw in the man's eyes.

"I knew it would be with you there." Satisfied, Mr. Dansick closed his eyes for a second. Then he remembered. "Did Bernie pick up his tie for the dance?" He spread his arms out toward the bureau in front of him. "Flowers, the nurses don't know where to put them anymore. And cards—look at them all." There must have been a hundred stacked on the night table next to the flowers and in packages by the bed.

Lee laughed. "You bet Bernie picked up his tie. A nice blue-and-red-striped one. And Mrs. Ross came in with a bright pink shirt. I sold her that rose tie you always said was made for a pink shirt."

"Oh, yes." Mr. Dansick laughed softly, then winced with pain and reminded himself not to laugh again.

"I guess you're busy." He looked at Lee's tired eyes. "Schoolwork and night work. Too much to ask of so young a boy."

But Lee shook his head. "No, not too much at all." He took the old man's hand. "Don't worry, I'm just fine."

Mr. Dansick leaned forward, using every bit of his strength to come closer to Lee. "Do you think, could you consider . . . ?" He groped for words that were eluding him. He lay back, exhausted, and tried again. "You're like a son to me, Lee. I don't have a son of my own. And the shop. Well, today people open chain stores. One shop. Who should care? But my shop," he said, pointing to his chest with the old look of pride, "it should go on." He looked at Lee, hoping that he was already anticipating what was to come. "I know you're young, but we could work together, and you could take over more and more, and eventually it would be yours." Mr. Dansick's words rushed out with genuine excitement.

"Whoa." Lee stopped him. "Look, Mr. Dansick, I have to graduate from school yet. It's only in a couple more months, but it's still in between me and any final decisions about what I'm going to do. Give me a little more time." He didn't bring up Michigan or his mother. Not now. Not with the bullet just fresh out of Mr Dansick's belly.

"Did they catch the guys?" he asked.

"Policemen here all the time." Mr. Dansick's hands circled the room. "All over. They sit and ask questions and leave and come back with nothing."

"Did you know them?"

"Now you sound like the policemen." Mr. Dansick frowned. "No. They were young, with hard looks, and eyes like glass marbles. No feeling. I remember thinking, They won't shoot. Not these kids. But the bullet was already burning into me while I thought this."

Lee could see that Mr. Dansick was tiring. "Look, I'd better go. I'll be back tomorrow. I just wanted you to know Harry's coming in during the day and I'm there when he isn't. Everyone up and down the block has been leaving good wishes and plants. Wait until you see the store. Boxes of candy, baskets of fruit. I'll bring some of them tomorrow."

Mr. Dansick nodded. "You keep some of it. Give away the food that will spoil. You know who'll need it." Then he said softly, "Lee, one time when I was young like you, I needed a job really bad. There was no money then. I was only thirteen, and my father said, 'It's time you helped bring in money.' So I went to apply for a job at a meat market. There had been an ad in the paper. A lot of people showed up. Many were older than I. Some even experienced. We all sat in the room outside, with straw, dust and dirt all over the floor, waiting for the butcher. While we were waiting, I looked at the floor and noticed that it probably had not been cleaned for days. I was only a kid, but the dirt bothered me, or maybe it was the fact that no one cared about it. There was a broom in the corner, so, with nothing better to do to pass the time, I got up and swept the floor. When the butcher came in, he noticed that the floor was clean. 'Who swept it?' he asked. 'I did,' I answered. 'You've got the job,' he said, just like that, without talking to any of the others who were now grumbling and leaving." He clutched Lee's hand, and his grasp was strong. "It's that something inside that doesn't wait to be asked. I had it. You have it." Mr. Dansick smiled proudly, remembering the moment long ago when he was thirteen. "You're like that, Lee. You take the broom. You know when the work has to be done, and you take pride in doing it. That can't be found just in any boy—or in any man."

Lee left the hospital knowing what Mr. Dansick was saying. If there was something special about Mr. Dansick, it wasn't how many degrees he had hanging on the wall or the size of his paycheck. The integrity came from that inner circle inside of him. Tonight Mr. Dansick had made him feel equal to anything.

He didn't go home. He drove by the ice cream shop, but didn't stop there, either. He knew Jo wasn't the answer tonight. He didn't feel like sharing his thoughts with her. He knew she wouldn't care to hear them.

He stopped at Rennie's house. Mrs. Jackson opened the door. "Hi, Lee." She was a little surprised. He wasn't dropping around as much lately and it was after ten.

"I know it's late," he said. "I just thought Rennie might be up."

"No," Mrs. Jackson said and shook her head. "She went to bed quite early tonight. In fact, I was surprised. I hope she's not getting sick."

"Well, she had archery practice today. That usually tires her out."

"Would you like to come in for a cup of coffee?"

"No. Thanks anyway, Mrs. Jackson. I'd better get home. Just tell her I stopped by. I'll see her in school tomorrow."

Rennie stood listening at the doorway to her bedroom. The braces, clear up her back and close to her skin, held her like a puppet as she listened to Lee talk to her mother. Then she heard the door shut.

She smiled in the dark. She could have come out, but she didn't want him to know. Not yet. She needed more time to practice walking without wobbling, to get her arms used to the crutches, her legs used to the stiffness and her body to become accustomed to the foreign weight that pushed against it.

She used the walking bar in her room, walking between it, back and forth. She continued her practice, trying to be quiet, not wanting her mother to know, wanting to keep the secret between her and the night until she was ready. It was strange to feel tall again and to look at things from above. Even looking down made her shaky.

Slowly, back and forth. Back and forth. Maybe this was the reason Lee had been cooling off. She had sensed a change in him these past weeks, and gradually she had come to realize that perhaps he really wanted her standing and walking. Perhaps his hints about her wearing braces had been more than just hints. Perhaps it had been an actual request.

She was heavy on the braces. Her height, and the fact that she was a big girl, didn't help. Many of the people she had known who had worn braces were of lighter weight.   They found braces easier than a wheelchair. For her, the braces had always been painful and awkward.

She did her toy soldier walk across the room. Perhaps Lee thought she didn't care enough about him to do something he wanted. Maybe that was what love was all about. Doing something for someone else that you wouldn't have done for yourself. Maybe there would be other nights like Bess's party, when the closeness between them meshed them into one. If he saw her try walking, perhaps he would be able to tell her what she was sure she could see in his eyes.

The door opened, and a beam of light came into the room. The light switched on. "Lee just came over . . ." The words stopped in midflight.

Rennie turned around. Her mother stood there a moment, stunned. "Rennie," she said.

Rennie tried to explain. "Look, I don't want anyone to know. I didn't even want you to know. Not until I was sure I could handle it."

"Rennie." Her mother just stood there, repeating her name, clasping her hands together, almost as though in prayer. A smile mixed with sobs crossed her lips, and she ran over to Rennie and threw her arms around her.

Rennie nearly toppled over. "Hold it," she said and laughed. "Mom, you're going to knock me over."

But her mother held her firmly in her arms, steadying her braces, holding her and sobbing and laughing at the same time, saying things that neither would remember later. "Rennie," she said at last, "Rennie, you're walking!"

Rennie let herself be held. It was funny. Standing there with the braces holding her up, with the pain still racking her body, she didn't feel like she was walking at all.

But she didn't tell her mother how she felt. Her mother had waited too long. Maybe Lee was right.

Maybe all of them were right. Maybe standing and walking would make the difference. And then they would all let her alone . . . so that she could get on with everyday living.

Truth
and Deception

"That cat ran away!" Bess's mother stood at the opened front door. It was seven-thirty in the morning, and the sun was just beginning to show itself in the sky.

Bess, dressed and ready to leave for school, quickly put her books down on the kitchen table. This meant that Puff—whom she kept like a treasure in the house, away from speeding cars and the woods across the street—Puff was lost.

"How did she get out?" Bess asked while she looked in the hall closet and under the living room couch.

Her mother shook her head. "She's not there. I looked already. I've looked all over the house. She must have gone out when your father left for work."

"But that was an hour ago." Bess put on her coat. "I've got to find her. It looks like it's going to snow. You know how she hates the cold."

Her heart was beating wildly as she ran down the street calling out Puff's name. Each bush looked like it could conceal the Persian cat. Suddenly, everything around her looked like a possible hiding place for Puff. Bess's eyes strayed to the woods across the street. She pictured the main highway behind the long scrawny trees. Quickly, she looked away. That would be later.

She'd face that after the homes and backyards and carports had been searched.

"Puff," her voice coaxed as she ran past patios and porches, looking behind garbage cans. The cat, pampered all these years, wasn't used to the outdoor sounds of automobiles racing by, of dogs barking threateningly, of winter winds.

A few snowflakes began to fall. "Oh, no," Bess moaned in the wind. Now in a panic, her calls grew frantic, and she raced against the white flakes that were whipping about her face and stinging her cheeks.

"Hey, where you rushing to? And you're going in the wrong direction. The bus is that way." Josh stood in front of her, the snowflakes dotting his blue jacket. For a moment, memories of her party, of Josh not coming, got in the way, and she started to walk past him. But he grabbed her arm and turned her around. "What's wrong, Bess?"

His eyes were so concerned that she couldn't be angry with him—not now, when fear of losing Puff blinded her eyes with tears.

"It's Puff. She ran away. I can't find her." She didn't care that tears were running down her cheeks or that her hair flew in every direction. Always before, when they spoke or met casually by the bus in the morning, she planned her words; her laugh was always so cheerful; and her hair was in place. She wanted to be everything she thought he wanted in a girl. She could do it from the neck up. She was sure of that. From the neck down were the pounds that proved to be another matter.

Today her appearance was unimportant. Only Puff mattered.

Josh looked around. "Where do you think she'd go? You know sometimes cats have their favorite places."

Bess put up her hands in defeat. "Anywhere. She's never been outside. I don't think she'd know how to get back home." She began to walk farther down the block. Josh walked with her.

"You'll be late for the bus," she cautioned.

"Don't worry about it," he said, as the wind picked up and carried his words away. "I have a calico cat. Old stray. He comes and goes but, well, he means a lot to me. I know how I'd feel if he didn't show up one day."

They spent the next hour searching around the split-level homes in the area. There were cats, beige and white and black, plenty of them, and they all seemed to come forth this morning, as though the word was out that Puff was among them, a cat of the street. They purred around Bess's legs, ran over garbage cans, whined from alleys, but they weren't Puff.

It seemed hopeless. The snow, now falling heavily and laying an even coating across the sidewalks, blinded them. Bess sat down on the curb. Another time she would have been running through the snow, feeling its coldness upon her face, or making snowballs. Now it was her enemy. She hated it. Tears, mixing with snow, were back on her cheeks. She was sure Puff would freeze to death.

"Look, maybe the SPCA picked her up, or maybe somebody just took her in because of the snow." He put his arm around her. "Come on, Bess. It's early yet." She felt his warmth even through his jacket. His arm enclosed her in a circle of understanding.

"I really love her," she said, unashamedly, with Josh wiping the snow away from her nearly frozen hands. "She's my second-best friend." She didn't care if he knew that. It seemed right that he did. The pretenses that she had so often worn when appearing in public were gone now. Only anguish and fear and a bit of fatigue were left. "I guess it must seem dumb to you, having a cat for a best friend. But aside from Rennie, she's the only one who really listens to what I have to say."

They began to walk down the street again, Josh guiding her, she leaning on his strength. "It's not silly," he said. "I think animals are special . . . and people who care about them are special, too."

She wasn't sure why they both happened to look up at the tree in Brady's backyard or if Puff's meow had alerted them. But there was Bess's cat, just high up enough to be afraid to jump down, hanging on with her claws against the wind that blew her fur up across her back. Bess ran to her, but it was Josh who was able to stretch and lift the cat off the cold limbs of the tree.

"I don't know how to thank you," she said, hugging Puff to her and warming her with her own body.

"That's a lucky cat," Josh said, as they hurried back down the block, "to be loved like that."

They left Puff happily curled near the heating vent of the kitchen. Bess's mother drove them to school.

"I've got to get to science class." Josh hurried into the hallway.

"Thanks again for caring." She never would have said that yesterday. Today it seemed important to say what she felt, not what she thought other people wanted to hear. They had shared a special time—she and Josh—and sharing brought with it truth.

"If I ever lose my calico, I'll know who to call."

"See you," she said and waved. Neither one had mentioned her birthday party. But after today, it seemed the birthday episode involved two other people, who really didn't know each other at all.

He answered, almost finishing her sentence, "At Rennie's party." She stood there for a second, stunned by the impact of his words. She had to find Rennie and tell her that Josh was coming to the party. "What are you doing New Year's Eve?" had become a familiar question during December. And Rennie had decided to give a party. She had invited several couples from school, the ones she had become friendly with at archery and swimming. And, of course, Lee. Rennie had argued with Bess and finally convinced her that Josh should be invited because he may have simply forgotten Bess's birthday party. And now he said he was coming, only this time, because of the way he had looked at her, it was different. No boy had ever looked at her in just that way before. But, then again, she had said things to Josh that day which she never let another boy know.

She hurried down the hall in search of the familiar wheelchair, and she found Rennie talking with Jo outside English class. Jo stood in front of Rennie's chair, almost blocking her way.

"I'm meeting Lee tonight," Bess heard Jo tell Rennie in her warm voice. "He's the greatest, isn't he?"

Rennie nodded, not noticing Bess off to the side.

"Do you know what I like most about him?" Jo went on, her rosebud mouth so innocent. "He's so kind. I never heard him say a mean word to anyone."

Bess watched, agonizing for her friend, as Rennie shifted in the chair. Jo kept her position in front of the chair.

"I think my class will be starting shortly. I don't want to be late," Rennie said, trying to end the conversation.

"Oh, you have a couple more minutes. You know," she went on, "I've really been quite understanding about Lee helping you out. Don't you think I have?"

Rennie looked up. Jo's rosebud mouth had turned ugly.

"I mean, driving you here and driving you there. But he's that kind of guy." Jo shifted the books under her arm. Her long legs changed position as she came closer to Rennie. "We've been dating quite a while," she said slowly. "For about a year. You might say we're going steady."

Bess saw the color leave Rennie's face. That was enough. She rushed over to the chair and pushed her way in front of Jo. "Hi," she said. "Aren't you late for science?" Then, without waiting for an answer, she put her own body between Rennie and Jo and began pushing the wheelchair down the hall.

"We're really quite proud of you, Lee and I," Jo called after them. "Keep up the good work."

Even though they were now far away from Jo, her words still stung.

Bess stopped the chair at the science class. "What was that all about?"

Rennie shook her head and took a deep breath. "I think she got the news about New Year's Eve. She knows Lee is coming to my party." Bess had never seen Rennie really tired until now. Rennie sat back in the chair, as though Jo's assault had drained her strength. "I can't blame her, really," Rennie said. "I would have felt the same way . . . I would feel the same way if someone took Lee away from me."

Bess waited a while, but somewhere between homework assignments and the science quiz, she told Rennie about Josh and Puff and New Year's Eve.

She went home with Rennie that afternoon after school. They had work to do to get Rennie ready for the big night. For the real purpose of the party—the one only Bess and Rennie's mother were aware of—was that Rennie would use her braces for the first time. Rennie put on her braces, then sat on the bed, her braces unlocked, her feet dangling. Bess looked out of the window at the snow capping the windowsills and the trees matted under the heaviness of white.

"How's it going?" she asked Rennie.

"One more week. That's all I have until New Year's. And it's rough. Sometimes I think maybe it's all wrong."

"What?" Bess asked her, not believing what she heard. "After all your work?"

Rennie stretched over and picked up the letter from Carol. She handed it to Bess.

Bess sat down on the bed next to her and read the letter aloud. She started with a cheerful voice, but her words grew serious.

Dear Rennie,

I can't believe they talked you into getting on those braces. I remember what you went through at the Rehab Center and sometimes I would feel so guilty, because it was easy for me to walk on braces, and so hard for you. Remember how sometimes I would take them off and say they bothered me, too, when they didn't, but the look on your face was too much for me to see? What are they doing to you, Rennie? Why have they made you feel that you will be special standing? You have to swing your legs when you walk, so it isn't as though it's a real walk. Rennie, think about it. Why does Lee have to have you standing? Aren't you good enough for him in a wheelchair?

As for me, I just got a job at a switchboard in an insurance company nearby. It looks good. It's my kind of work and the people here have been great. Rennie, I've been in a chair much longer than you. Using braces has to be for the right reasons and for the right people. Does Lee really feel that standing will make you more of a person?

                              I am your friend,
                                    Carol

Bess let out her breath almost in a gasp. She kept staring and rereading the letter because the words were harsher than anything she would have dared to say to Rennie. Yet she recognized that they held some truth and that they were from a friend who cared deeply if Rennie was hurt. She would rather hurt herself in a lesser way and prevent a deeper hurt later. Could she tell Rennie that she agreed with Carol? Could she tell her that, from the beginning, she had nagging doubts about the big surprise? Standing on braces would not change Rennie, the beautiful Rennie. From whatever position she faced life, sitting or standing, she was unbeatable.

Rennie saved her from the decision. She got up, locked her braces, took her crutches and swung over to the walking bars. "Let's go," she said. "Time me." No mention of the letter was made the rest of the evening, as the sound of crutches and braces filled the room. Bess had never seen such determination as she saw in Rennie that evening, and a persistent guilt stayed with her all the way home. How many times had she said, "I can't. I can't cut down on my eating. I can't resist the chocolate cake. I can't lose weight." Still remembering the sound of the braces going back and forth, the picture of Rennie's face set with stubbornness still clear in her mind, the memory of her own words, "I can't," made her cringe inside herself.

Then, just before she was to go to bed, her stomach began to growl with hunger. The dreaded growl that always pushed her to the refrigerator grew stronger. A bewildering feeling of frustration and loneliness crept over her. Bess cleaned up her room, hung all the clothes draped over the clothes rack in the closet, picked out her clothes for the next day. The nail polish bottles lined up on the floor next to her bed were put on the bookshelf, and she stacked the books neatly on the night table beside her bed. She put the balls of wool that she had been using to crochet an afghan for Rennie's wheelchair back in the big bag in the closet. Then, unable to fight it any longer, the hunger still gnawing at her stomach, she ran downstairs and opened the refrigerator.

It had been a hard day. She had spent much of her energy searching for Puff and even more after school with Rennie and her attempts to walk. But none of them was here now . . . not Josh and his warm smile, not Rennie and her strength, not even Puff who was still recovering from her excursion into the outside world, huddling in a soft living room chair.

A piece of chocolate cake sat there, left over from her mother's bridge party. Bess took a deep breath. She knew she had been losing weight, because she had been kept too busy to have any interest in snacks, and she could feel the difference.

She looked at the cake again and remembered Josh sitting at the curb with her. But his face grew fainter and Rennie's encouraging words weaker as the chocolate cake sat there. She had to stop that growling inside her stomach. The cake would do it. She put the cake on the kitchen table, grabbed a glass of milk, took out a knife from the drawer and cut herself a big piece. She took a forkful of cake and felt its delicious sweetness flow through her mouth. And then, right there in the middle of the first bite, she saw Rennie, wincing, locking the braces and walking back and forth, trying for New Year's. It was as though Rennie were there looking over her shoulder now. Would she say, "Bess, you coward, you powerless coward"? Would she want her for a friend, with a mouthful of cake and no guts?

The cake felt dry in her mouth, dry and sour and tasteless. She could barely swallow that first mouthful. Bess quickly took the cake plate and put it back in the refrigerator. She took the piece that she had cut off and threw it down the garbage disposal, then she turned on the disposal and listened as the noise swallowed it up. Her face was flushed, and her heart was beating as fast as Rennie's must beat each day when she struggled with her braces. What the heck was life all about if you couldn't fight your own battles?

Bess could see her mother sitting in the living room, watching TV. Her knitting was in her lap. She looked tired. Suddenly, Bess felt sorry for her mother, sorry because she had spent so many years calling doctors and talking about the same boring subject of Bess being overweight. It didn't seem fair to have to face the same old problem summer after summer, winter after winter. Problems, at least, should change. Rennie had once told her, "I don't mind if it's all uphill. As long as the hills change." Bess could see herself next year and the year after, with the same problem of overeating. Not growing, not changing, not fighting back, not knowing the excitement that Rennie was experiencing even now, in trying to change her life.

Bess walked past her mother, then stopped at the first step leading to the upstairs bedrooms. "I threw some cake down the garbage disposal. I didn't eat it," she said clearly and slowly, with a sense of pride, as though she were making a great proclamation.

Her mother looked up, surprised at what Bess had said. She was even more surprised at the look she saw in her daughter's eyes.

Stand Up
to Be Counted

"Jo called."

As Lee was straightening his tie, his mother came up behind him and said in the voice of a stranger, "Jo called." His eyes didn't leave the mirror.

"She wants to talk to you. Although I doubt if anyone can talk to you lately."

"I have Rennie's party tonight," he answered.

"Jo said it was important. She said to meet her at the ice cream shop at eight-thirty. I think you owe her that . . . don't you, Lee? After all those months."

His mother was in Jo's corner, in any corner other than Rennie's. Lee looked at his watch. The party was called for nine o'clock. It didn't give him much time. Less than an hour. He put on his jacket, straightened the collar of his shirt and took his wallet from the top of the bureau.

"I don't want to talk about it." He took his shoes from the closet and looked them over. Then, realizing they needed a shine, he went into the bathroom and took out the shoe polish kit from the bathroom cabinet. His mother followed him. The bathroom was small, too small to contain rising tempers.

"Do you know what I think?" She didn't wait for

or expect an answer. "I think you've decided not to go away to school because of Rennie. I think you pity her, and have lost all perspective. She's a crippled girl, Lee. All your life you'd have to take care of her. Do you know what it's like to have someone dependent on you like that? Don't you want a family, a normal life? She's an invalid, Lee."

Lee polished his shoes harder. Rennie, an invalid. Rennie swimming in the pool at school, her body so free and graceful. Rennie shooting those arrows beyond many of the other archers' endurance. Rennie wheeling through the school halls, making friends, talking about the future with enthusiasm that spread like wildfire to those around her. Rennie, who loved children and caught their conversation in a web of excitement that drew them to her.

He and Rennie had spoken once about children. Sitting on the edge of the tub, bending down to make the shine come clearer, he tried to remember. It seemed important to remember their conversation now, to blot out his mother's words that kept attacking him.

One day, he had come over and she was baby-sitting for a niece. She had held the little girl on her lap, fed her, changed her diaper. He had watched her.

"Someday I'd like to have that kind of family," she had said, looking into the carriage. She had seen the question in his eyes. "I can have children," she said. "But, heck, I don't want to wear a sign telling everyone." And then she had looked at him mischievously. "You don't, do you?"

They had laughed together, with the little girl snuggling between them. He had felt relieved, although he didn't know why he should be glad that she could have kids. Some people got married and couldn't have them even when they were able to walk. That day, somewhere in his mind, he had said the word "married." It had scared him. He had been scared ever since.

He looked up at his mother, his face red from bending and from the effort of keeping back his anger. He stretched out his long legs and put on his shoes. "My decision," he said at last slowly, "not to go to college is my decision. I'll go to school at night. There's a lot I want to learn. But, truthfully, I can learn it right here. It doesn't necessarily have to be in Michigan."

"How do you know? You haven't even given it a chance."

He stood up, towering over her. "Because I know now that I have what I want."

"A tie shop and an invalid." The ruthlessness of the words even caught his mother by surprise, and she looked up at him in dismay. For a moment, she put out her hand, as though to sweep the words back.

It was too late. "An invalid." Lee pushed her aside firmly as he went to the sink to wash his hands. Unable to believe that the harsh words had come from his own mother, he felt a need to retaliate. "What are you worried about, really? Are you worried about Rennie and me, or what people will think about Rennie and me?"

"And what will they think? They'll think something's wrong with your head, that's what. Mr. Dansick has been unfair, putting the burden of the shop on you. Don't you understand that you're ruining your life?"

Where had this heartlessness been buried all these past years? Where had this anger been hidden, dormant, unspoken? Did it take a person like Rennie to bring it all to the surface? "You're right about one thing," Lee said, leaving the bathroom. "It's my life. And there are two people in my life that I wouldn't part with. I've learned more from them than I've learned from anyone or anything else in my whole life. I could go to Michigan or travel all over this country, and never—do you understand this?—never find two people like them again."

"You could come back to Rennie, later, and the

tie shop, too." She wasn't giving in. "Don't throw your whole life away because of pity."

There was the word again, shaped like a bullet, only this time it landed in his chest and blew him apart. He pitied himself sometimes because he felt half Rennie's worth. He pitied all the people who looked away from her, who never got to know her. He pitied his mother most of all because she didn't understand that in Rennie she could have found a friend.

He left her standing by the sink in the bathroom, her face ghostly, speechless, although her mouth was slightly open. He didn't say he was sorry, as he had said so often during the past weeks. He let what he had said stay. And so did she. Neither one wanted to retract what was said.

Lee slammed the front door behind him. He drove over to the ice cream shop. Jo was waiting for him outside. Light snow was beginning to fall, and it frosted her hair and crept around her shoes. She seemed to shiver there under the light. Lee honked the horn and she ran over to the car.

He had left the motor running, as though to tell her that this was a brief stop.

"How could you?" She turned to him. "I didn't think you would go until tonight. Not until this very last moment did I think you would go to that party."

"I told you two weeks ago."

She shook her head. "I know. But I thought you felt sorry for her. I thought, maybe you didn't know how to say no, but that you'd find a way."

Lee turned off the motor and turned toward Jo. She didn't give him a chance to speak. She threw her arms around him and pressed her body closer to his, and the scent of lemon shot up his nostrils as her hands floated around his shoulders. He pushed her hands away.

"Does she do all of this to you?" She looked at him and kissed his neck and did the things she knew

aroused him. She had done her homework where he
was concerned. "Can she . . . can she . . . ?" She held
his face in her hands, and her mouth, soft and eager,
caught his again and again.

"Look," he said, holding her hands in his. "I've got
to get going. I'm sorry about tonight." He touched
her cheeks. Don't ask me anything now. I have no
straight answers."

"Lee," she said, and tugged at his elbow as he turned
on the motor. "What can she give you—a whole life of
wheeling her around? She's not even a whole woman."
Another bullet, and it sent him spinning. He looked
at Jo. He couldn't give her an answer that would make
sense. Not now. He couldn't tell her that he thought
Rennie was more of a woman than anyone he had
ever met. He didn't want to hurt her by telling her
that celebrating a New Year's Eve would be nothing
if he weren't with Rennie. A couple of months ago
it wouldn't have mattered. But each day it seemed to
matter more. "Look," he said, glancing at his watch,
"I have to get going. I'll call you during the week.
We'll talk then."

It seemed to satisfy her. "OK," she said. "I did
make plans to go to Barney Blake's party. You didn't
expect me to sit home, did you?" She looked over her
shoulder and flashed her special smile. "I hope you
have as good a time as I'll have tonight." She let him
figure out the meaning for himself.

Walking up Rennie's driveway, he couldn't understand why everyone was fighting so hard to keep the
two of them apart when they weren't even together.
Nothing serious had ever been said between them. No
commitment. She was a girl, like any other girl. They
had gone to one party together. A couple of rides in
the car on Sunday. Not even a real date. He had never
really taken her out. He wasn't quite sure where he
could even take her with the wheelchair, or why he
had never tried. Which restaurant, which movie was

accessible? Could she get inside the bowling alley or the soda shop? Would her wheelchair fit through the doorway? He hadn't asked her. He would be ashamed to admit to her that he didn't know. Lee brushed away the questions in his mind and rang Rennie's doorbell.

Rennie answered it. The usual smile was gone from her face. "I was worried," she said. "Were you busy at the tie shop?"

He didn't answer. He had never lied to her, never had a reason to. Yet he knew this wasn't the time to explain his meeting with Jo. He didn't understand it himself.

Bess saved him from any reply. She held Josh's hand as she hurried toward them. "Doesn't the room look great? Lee, give me your coat. Wait till you taste the punch."

"How's Mr. Dansick?" Josh asked as he led Lee to the sandwich tray on the dining room table. Lee looked back at Rennie. She seemed to disappear somewhere between the crepe paper lining the ceiling and the balloons that bounced from the walls. Several of the kids from school circled her wheelchair, and the doorbell kept ringing. Josh scooped out a drink from the big punch bowl on the table. Sandwiches were lined like tiny soldiers in a big parade across the dining room table.

"Mr. Dansick's coming along fine," Lee said in between mouthfuls.

Music from the hi-fi set everyone in motion. Rennie wheeled up alongside him. "Come on," she said as she grabbed his hand, "let's dance."

Lee hesitated, unprepared for her request, again angry at himself for always being in the position of not being sure whether she was kidding.

"I'm a rotten dancer," he said, hedging.

"So follow me," she said, knowing he was being untruthful, and that determined look was on her face again, the look he had seen so often in archery, the expression that shot into her eyes at the bottom of those steps at school each morning.

"You stand there. I'll sit here. Now, just pretend I'm a little higher up." She laughed at his awkwardness. The music was the kind that could be danced apart, fast, full of rhythm, but he stood there unable to move his feet.

Rennie began to sway to the music, her shoulders keeping time, her arms picking up the beat of the music. He began to move with her, entranced by her blonde hair, like flashes of gold, falling this way and that. Now and then she would move the wheelchair closer, then farther away, and, as the music got louder and faster, Lee forgot Jo and his mother and the fact that Rennie was sitting. She had such rhythm. It seemed to flow through her fingers and long arms. He realized she must have been a great dancer before . . . How he wished his mother could see them now. Flashes of the early part of the evening cut into his mind, and again he fought against the anger that kept rising within him.

They sat on the side with some of the other couples during the slow dances. Bess and Josh never sat down. Bess looked trim in her dark blue dress. Her face had lost some of its chubbiness, and her hair was swept back.

"Bess looks so good," Rennie said proudly as she slid onto the couch and Lee sat down beside her. They had paper plates with stacks of sandwiches on their laps.

"Didn't you eat dinner?" She watched Lee gulp down one sandwich after the other.

"Didn't have time to eat tonight." He didn't tell her he was too busy fighting. "Kept the shop open a little later. Last-minute ties for New Year's. Mr. Greenwood ran in. He spilled something on his tie at dinner and wanted a special purple replacement. And then Bob Jenson—you know, that kid who lives upstairs from the store—well, he ran down. Seems he had his first date tonight. He'd hustled some newspapers and had an extra buck. And that's what happened to my dinner."

"And Mr. Dansick?"

"He's home now. Looking better, too. His sister seems like a great person. She wants him to come out to California next year, for a while, so she can take care of him. She can only stay up here for a couple more months."

"What do you think he'll do?"

Lee shrugged. "Beats me." But really he knew, and she knew, too. He'd want Lee to run the store.

"At thirteen a Jewish boy becomes a man," Mr. Dansick had said to Lee last night. "So why not all boys? At seventeen, you've been a man for a long time."

"What are you going to do?" Rennie asked him, the concern showing in her eyes that grew dark. The unspoken word between them, unspoken as all the other words were, seemed to slip from her lips. "What about Michigan?"

"Don't want to talk about it now. It's New Year's Eve." Balloons broke and horns tooted, and everyone sang out at once. Lips touched one another, and the New Year broke joyously in the Jackson living room.

It was midnight, and she was in his arms at last. There on the couch, he had turned to her and kissed her for the first time amid thirty screaming, laughing, dancing, well-wishing friends.

The party broke up late. Mr. and Mrs. Jackson had long since gone to bed, satisfied that the party was a success and that the food would not run out. Everyone seemed reluctant to leave, but finally only Bess and Josh remained.

"Well," Bess said, her face flushed with happiness, "it was just a perfect New Year's Eve." She meant it. She had cornered Rennie during the evening and told her she hadn't eaten any junk, just half a sandwich and a little soda. And when Josh had coaxed her to eat more, she had looked him straight in the eye and said, "I'm on a diet."

"We'll come over tomorrow," Josh said as he helped Bess on with her coat. "I think your parents will need some help in cleaning up." Josh looked back at the living room with confetti and broken balloons everywhere, and the paper dishes scattered all over the dining area.

"Thanks to both of you, and we'd love some help tomorrow," Rennie said.

Then the door shut behind them, and she and Lee were left alone in the room. At last. Rennie had hoped it would turn out this way. They had to be alone for her surprise. "I'll be right back," she said, as he stretched his long arms and leaned back on the couch.

Rennie wheeled into her bedroom where she had left the braces lying on the bed. Slowly, carefully, she undressed and then put on her braces, locking them. She straightened her clothes again and swung down the steps and toward the living room. She tried to remember only one thing—not Carol's letter, not her mother's persistence—but that Lee wanted it this way. For whatever reason, he thought it was best. She walked slowly down the hallway, swinging her legs as she went.

He turned around when he heard the swish of her skirt and saw her standing there in front of him, tall and slim, just standing there, the crutches under her armpits, an impish smile on her face.

He jumped up from the couch. "Rennie," he said, "Rennie." Then he took her in his arms, crutches, braces and all, and hugged her. He felt the steel up her back and the steel against his legs as he pressed her body to his.

He let go and looked at her. He didn't realize there would be so much steel encasing her and holding her up. Yet, she stood there, almost as tall as he was, her green eyes looking into his, and in that moment, as though a wave had rushed them, braces, wheelchairs, crutches were washed away. All that remained was their love.

Her circled her in his arms again. They stood that way for a long time.

The Breakup

Dear Carol,

I haven't heard from you in a while. How's your job? I guess you're too busy now to even write.

I suppose you want to know about Lee and me. Well, I wish I could tell you. These past months have just flown by. He's working so hard lately. I barely see him. And when I do, I don't know how to put this, but it's not me. You know, I wear the braces whenever I'm with him, but I can't do anything. I mean, we've never gone bowling and I couldn't bowl with the braces anyway. I couldn't even be comfortable in archery. I'm always so stiff, so sore, and even though I'm standing, well, I feel as if it's somebody else standing because I don't feel free.

But Lee seems so happy when he sees me in them. And I know he isn't seeing Jo anymore. I can tell by the way she passes me by in school and won't even turn my way. I'm sorry for her. I hate to hurt anybody, but I just love him so.

We still don't go out much. It's really my fault

now. I just don't feel steady or at ease without the chair. You know, I can move around so fast in the wheelchair. This is so different.

I don't know, Carol. I want to be happy because Mom is so happy and she's crazy about Lee, probably because he got me out of the chair. But me. I'm not happy, not the way I used to be.

Lee's so distant sometimes. He treats me like I'm glass. All I want to do is be in his arms, but his kisses are just goodnight, so long, as if he's afraid. Does he think I'm different?

She put the letter away, unfinished. She'd write the end to it another time.

The winter snows, so difficult for her to travel in, were gone, and the leaves were beginning to turn green, as the April sun grew stronger and stronger. It was a warm day, an unusually warm day for April. About seventy-five degrees, the radio had said. Rennie sat by the window in her wheelchair wondering what the summer would hold. A foreboding sadness seemed to cling to her lately. Free-moving Rennie. Where had she gone? Her arms and legs were tired. Her body seemed heavier, more burdensome than it had been before.

She looked at the braces over in the corner. They would be good occasionally. But she had a feeling that Lee wanted them for always. She cringed thinking about it.

The doorbell rang. She heard Lee's voice and started to wheel out of the room. Then she remembered. Quickly she put on her "hardware," as she liked to call it. Her mother and Lee were in the midst of a conversation when she came in.

"Boating," she heard. And then her mother looked over toward Rennie.

"Boating. You want to go rowboating?"

"On the lake," Lee said. "It's just beautiful out today. Harry came in and relieved me, and the boats are ready. You said you were a good swimmer. She's not just joking, is she, Mrs. Jackson?"

Mrs. Jackson laughed. "No, Lee. She really is good. I'd trust her on the water anytime. She might wind up saving you."

"Well, I can't go like this," Rennie said. "Look, let me change and I'll get the wheelchair."

She saw Lee's eyes change mood. She explained a little haughtily, "I'd like to be comfortable in the rowboat. All this hardware will make us sink."

She was joking, but somehow the joke had been turned on her. She went back into the bedroom and changed into a pair of shorts and a jersey top. Then she got into the wheelchair and joined Lee in the living room.

Once in the car, Rennie's mood passed. She forgot everything but the beautiful day. She moved closer to Lee. He looked over at her. She let her hand rest near his elbow. Each time she moved toward him she felt that he moved away.

The lake was empty. Just the ducks and swans, quacking in circles, kept them company.

Lee untied the rowboat from the dock. "I know it's a little early," he said. "But that's the way I like it. When the weather gets warmer, we won't even be able to get a boat."

He took a long look at the boat and then at Rennie, still on the land. "Come on," he said, "this is a whole new ball game." He lifted her from the chair, and they were in the boat. She was in his arms, holding him around the neck, and he was wobbling back and forth, as the boat shuddered from the weight of the two of them. Gently, he put her down on the seat, and she rested against the cushion in the boat.

He grabbed the set of oars and began to row toward the middle of the lake. The boat took on speed, gliding across the lake, scattering the swans, with birds flying up to the clouds. Rennie's eyes traveled toward the birds and the clouds. White and puffy, they were moving overhead quickly. Off in the distance, darker clouds were gathering.

"Rain," she said, looking back at Lee. She let her fingers make tiny trails through the water.

"Want to go back?" he asked cautiously. But she didn't want to be cautious today. If she were Jo, and there was no wheelchair resting on the dock, would he have suggested going back so soon?

"Let's keep going right to the center," Rennie said firmly.

About twenty minutes later, they stopped at the center of the lake. The oars lay at the side of the boat. The water below them stirred and moved the boat up and down in a gentle swaying motion.

He was sitting back just looking at her. "Do you know your nose is burning?" he asked.

"I tan easily."

They talked about tans and sunshine and water for a while. "Rennie," he said, and his voice grew quieter, "I spoke to Mr. Dansick last night."

She didn't look at him, focusing her eyes on the long neck of the pretty white swan gliding by so perfectly, as though it appeared on cue.

"I said yes."

She stopped looking at the swan. "You did?" she said, while all her pulses seemed to take off in a wild symphony of their own, beating madly.

"I told him I'd stay." Lee began to row again, turning the boat toward shore. "He said he'll wait until I graduate in June. Then he'll go back with his sister for a couple of months, to get on his feet. He wants me to run the shop. I'll get a raise and go to school at night. There'll be a bonus and all kinds of benefits, and a percentage of the profit. If I'm still interested in a year or two and I want to buy into the business, well, it's up to me. I don't know what I'll feel like then, but now, it looks good."

Rennie smiled. "I'm so happy for you, Lee. I'm glad you have what you want."

"I really don't have that fine line of ambition my father had, Rennie. He worked day and night as an accountant, and during the tax season we never saw him. Books were always on his bed or in the living room. First an accountant, then a CPA. Always more and more money. He wanted it. It made him happy. I remember him, always pouring over his bookkeeping. So he died a young man, and he left us a lot of insurance. I think I want more than that."

She listened and loved him.

"I can't seem to go for the package deal. I want to keep changing, go for different things. But they're just not the things I can explain. They don't really make much sense."

"It makes sense to me," Rennie said.

He looked over at her. The wind picked up as the dark clouds moved closer over their heads. They didn't notice the change in weather, nor that the sun had dimmed and a darkness had crept over the lake. Even the swans stopped their noises and edged their way toward shore. A shadow of an oncoming storm covered the edges of the lake.

He had put his oars down for a second, and she was letting her hands drift through the water when, to their surprise, a gust of wind set the lake in a frenzied motion, curling the water into little waves that churned under the boat, then tipped it.

"Rennie!" She heard his frantic call.

"I'm OK," she said. "Come on." The shore was not too far off, and she began to swim toward it.

Laughing, she dragged herself up on the grass, a little winded, water dripping from her shorts, her jersey clinging to her. Her breasts, full and womanly, curved under the wet jersey, and she lay on her back, taking in deep breaths.

Lee fell down beside her. "Oh, boy." He was laughing and coughing up water and holding his stomach. "Leave it to us."

He turned over, leaning on his elbow. "Are you all right?" He looked down at her, his eyes so close to her, his mouth even nearer, water dripping down his forehead.

She pulled his head down and kissed him, turning her body toward him. There were no braces between them now, no wheelchair in the way. Just the two of them, toe to toe.

He kissed her back, and his arms went around her. She felt his body press her with wetness clinging between them. They were oblivious of the wind and of the storm. There were just the two of them, on the grass, learning the touch of one another.

And then he let her go and he was almost shaking. "I'm sorry," he said.

"Sorry? About what?"

"I shouldn't have."

"Shouldn't have what?" Rennie felt anger replace passion, and she lay there as he sat up, not facing her.

"Taken advantage of you. I shouldn't have."

The words set off an explosion inside her. "I could have said no," she said.

"It wasn't fair. I just shouldn't have tried . . ." He shook his head, looking down at the ground and fingering the grass.

She pulled herself up to a half-sitting position, still leaning on her elbows. "Why do you treat me this way?" Now, Carol's words floated back to her. "Freak." Haunting words. "Stay in your place. Don't dare it."

She dared. She dared it and now. "Why?" she asked louder. "Would you say these things to Jo?"

He looked at her. "Now hold it, Rennie. You're talking about apples and pears."

"Well, which am I? Pears or apples. I'll be whatever Jo is." She was beyond caring if her words hurt or not. "What am I to you?" She looked at him, her eyes steady. "Am I Rennie in a wheelchair, or Rennie to take to a party or a lake where no one else is? Am I someone you have to apologize to for touching? Just what am I to you?"

"Look, don't get angry." He tried to appease her. "I don't want to upset you." But the more he tried to calm her, the more upset she got.

"Upset me. Go ahead. I won't break." She was trembling now, and her legs began to spasm. She held them in place, damning them for their timing. He tried not to notice. "Come on, forget that my legs shake. Just talk, damn it, Lee. What do you think? That all my feelings were killed when they left my legs? Don't you realize that I want you, too?"

"Look, Rennie, please."

"Well, I do. I have feelings, and I want you to touch me. Don't you want to?"

"I'm sorry." Her honesty embarrassed him.

"Don't say that. I don't want to hear you're sorry again. I don't need your pity."

"Now hold it. I didn't say a thing about pity." Now he was getting angry. She was glad. At least he could dignify her with that emotion.

"It's in your eyes. Poor Rennie. Don't kiss her too much or she'll get up her hopes. And then what? Could the poor girl stand rejection? Reject Jo and she can take it. Right? But someone in a wheelchair? Go easy. Right?"

Now his eyes were inflamed, and he answered her, "Listen, you, as far as I'm concerned, you're tougher than anyone I've ever met. Sometimes I think you're tougher than I am. So don't go on about pity. I won't hear any more of it."

"Why? Does it kill you to face the truth? And while we're talking about truth, let's pull the whole drawer out."

"What do you mean by that?" He turned toward

her. There was a stillness between them, except for the breaking of the storm, which frightened both of them.

But Rennie couldn't stop now. "You couldn't take me in the wheelchair, could you?" Her voice was quiet. There was a finality about it that shook Lee. "You had to have me standing. Why? Would it have been easier when I met your mother again? Would it have been easier to take me to the movies or out to dinner?"

It began to rain. He couldn't tell if it was rainwater or tears that streamed down Rennie's face. "You don't have to answer that one," she said at last. "I know now what your reason was. You want me standing so that you can handle the situation in front of other people." Then she shook her head, and her wet hair began to curl. "Well, I tried it your way. It's not me. I'm not there. I wanted you so much I was willing to do anything, to become anybody you wanted."

Then she turned away as though she spoke to him through miles of forest. "No more," she said. "From now on I'm going to be me. She pulled herself along the grass to the wheelchair and got in. Then she wheeled back to the car and left him sitting there.

It hurt him to see her on the ground like that. But the worst part about the day, the terrible thing about it all, was that most of what she said was the truth. Lee knew that. And the truth sickened him. He wanted Rennie on those braces, not because of what it could do for her, but because of what it did for him. He couldn't forgive himself for that.

Even Lions Cry

When Rennie came home, she took the braces from her bed and put them in the closet. Just like that. If he won't have me any other way, then he won't have me, she said to herself. She closed the closet door and felt as though she were closing a chapter in her life.

Rennie didn't go to school the next day. "I'm not feeling well," she told her mother. She stayed in bed under the blankets and smelled spring flowers blooming in the backyard.

She grabbed a piece of scratch paper off the top of her desk.

Dear Carol,

You're right. You've been right all along. He was ashamed of me. He couldn't face it. He just didn't have the guts. And I was stupid, stupid, stupid.

That's all she could write because the tears were streaming down and it had all been said.

"Won't you have something to eat?" her mother pleaded at lunch, but Rennie shook her head. "Upset stomach," she said.

If her mother didn't believe her, she didn't show it.

She had noticed the braces in the closet. "Did something happen with Lee?" she asked toward dinner.

The sound of his name jarred Rennie, but she shook her head. She'd have to get used to hearing the name and accept the fact that it didn't fit into the picture of her life anymore. She'd have to get used to the feeling that he was in another world, circling hers, passing by. She'd just have to. "No," she said. "Nothing happened. I'm just not up to par."

The second day, her mother wanted to call the doctor. "You have archery," she said. "I don't think you've missed a session."

"Well, there's always the first time." She turned toward the wall, shutting her mother out.

The third day, an explanation was in order. Her mother sat by her bed in the morning. "You don't have any fever," she said.

"Good."

"You even look fine, except for those red eyes."

Rennie turned away.

"Are you going to talk about it, Rennie?"

"Don't ask me. Just don't open up the bag."

"Look. If you're ill, I'll have to call the doctor. If you're not, well, I'm not going to let you lie in bed all week. You're missing your studies, and it's near the end of the term. Rennie, tell me what's wrong."

"I don't think I can."

"It must be about Lee."

It was, and it wasn't. It was about everything. It was about her mother and the way she looked at Rennie. It was about her father, who wasn't there anymore . . . it was about all the people like her and the fact that all she wanted to do was to be happy. Couldn't they let her be happy?

"I'm worried about you." Her mother pushed back Rennie's hair and looked at her.

"The only thing you're worried about, the only

thing you've ever been worried about for the last two years is whether I'll walk again." Rennie flung the angry words at her mother. "Isn't that all that really counts to you? Well." She folded her hands over her face so that the sorrow wouldn't show. "You can stop worrying right now. This is it. You can't help me, because you're just like Lee. You can't face me in here, either." She patted the wheelchair. "Isn't it amazing?" She looked down at the blankets, talking to herself mostly, or perhaps to Carol, miles away, who knew the truth. "The two people who you think would understand, the two people closest to me, don't really understand at all. They're all the way on the other side."

Her mother left the room without a word and closed the door behind her.

That afternoon Bess came over. She knocked at the bedroom door. "It's me," she called.

"I don't feel like company," Rennie answered.

The door opened. "Boy, you really listen." Rennie looked cross.

"Nope, I never listen. That's been my big problem." Bess plopped down on the bed.

"I didn't invite you in." Rennie put on a sour face and tried to stare Bess down. But she couldn't. Bess's smile was bright and determined.

"I hear you're sulking," she said.

"No. I just don't feel well."

"Baloney! I know what happened. Your mother told me you had a fight with Lee."

"I don't want to talk about it." Rennie lay down, turned her back to Bess and pulled the covers over her shoulders.

Bess pulled an apple out of her pocketbook and began to munch on it. The crunching noise got Rennie to sit up again. "You're eating again." She said it crossly, as a reprimand.

But Bess shoved it off. "Yup. But only good stuff.

Lost five pounds last week. Here." She took out an apple and handed it to Rennie.

The slurping noises Bess made were too much to resist. Rennie bit into the apple.

"Well," Bess said, "what's the scoop?" She tried to sound light, but her heart ached for her friend. She had been worrying so much about Rennie these past few days. It was such a tough break, loving someone, and having it end somewhere in the middle.

Munching the apple, watching Rennie chew away at hers like a fallen warrior, she thought about the pounds that were slipping off her, little by little. Even the kids at school were beginning to notice. It was because of Rennie. All of it. Just being in the company of so much courage, some of it had to rub off.

It was the first time in Bess's life that she could remember thinking about something besides herself. Perhaps that was it. All the doctors and camps and mysterious prescriptions couldn't tell her that she had to think of something else besides her stomach. And she had to fight all the time. Fight back when frustration drove her to the refrigerator. Fight like Rennie fought. What a teacher she had! She looked at Rennie. The fighter looked a bit beaten now, and a little out of breath.

"Why did he have to make such a deal about my standing up? Why did he have to encourage me and take an interest in me and drive me here and drive me there? Why did he have to go halfway? I thought there was more to him. I thought he had so much more."

"Look," Bess said, trying to comfort her, "he's had a pretty mixed-up year. That whole tie shop has been on his shoulders, and there's his mother."

But Rennie turned toward her bitterly. "How could you understand? You're not in a wheelchair. You don't know how I feel." Rennie threw the apple core in the trash can and turned away from Bess.

Bess felt rejected. Their friendship, all they had been through together the past year, seemed to evaporate with Rennie's accusation, "You're not in a wheelchair." But the look in Rennie's eyes was like that of a wounded animal caught with an arrow in her belly, running, attacking blindly. Rennie was mixed up, and Bess knew that, when you get mixed up, sometimes you do just the opposite of what you want. She remembered eating the cake when she really wanted to throw it away. Those were the mixed-up days.

"What do you have against me just because I can walk? Huh? All this big talk about treating you as an equal and like anybody else. All you kept saying over and over is that you're like any other girl."

"I meant it."

"Well, get off that darn bed, then. Because if you could walk and you were Jo, well, she might spend about a day mooning over it, and she might cry every night in her room, but I'm sure she wouldn't lay around in bed for three days letting everyone know how much she was hurt. Now, I'm asking you, is this what happens when someone in a wheelchair is turned off, when they don't get what they want?"

Shocked, Rennie just stared at Bess. Never had Bess talked to her that way. There was no time to answer. Bess picked up her books and walked out of the room. Then she stuck her head back in the doorway quickly. "I'll be by to pick you up tomorrow. It's beautiful outside, and we can wheel to school." And then she was gone.

Rennie lay in bed that night and, while the moon led pathways to her room, she suddenly remembered the story her archery coach had once told her. All the archers had been lined up. One archer, exceptionally better than the others, kept hitting bull's-eye after bull's-eye. "How do you get to be so good?" she had asked. "Practice," he answered. "And that extra ingredient. The difference between those who just shoot and those who shoot to win is that the champion has to have the heart of a lion." The words "heart of a lion" stayed with her—soothing her and challenging her all at once. Rennie turned over and closed her eyes. She'd show them. She'd show them what the lionhearted could do.

The next morning she was dressed and waiting for Bess. Spring, with its smell of fresh grass, was all around them, and Rennie wheeled herself, while Bess carried the books.

"I'm sorry about yesterday and everything I said," Rennie apologized. "It's not fair just to strike out at anybody when you're angry."

Bess agreed. "We do a lot of unfair things to people sometimes, Rennie, and later we can't understand why." She was thinking of her mother and all those wasted, taunting years.

They reached the front steps of the school. Rennie saw Lee—though he wasn't really there—carrying her up, remembering the first time, way back somewhere, when the year was new and they had so much to learn about each other. Mr. Greenwood, the biology teacher, came down with the maintenance man. Rennie's heart sank. All her promises to herself seemed to fly away.

Bess whispered behind her, "He could be sick or something. Will you be OK?" They were in the main hall now. "I have a class at the other end." She wished she could stay with Rennie and see her through the whole day.

"What do you think I am, an invalid?" Rennie laughed, a little of the old spirit coming back to her. She took Bess's hand. "Thanks," she said. "I needed you today."

Bess smiled. Being needed was beautiful. It was even better than eating.

Rennie watched Bess run down the hall. Her legs, once so broad, were slimmer now, and the skirt swishing wasn't as bulky. Rennie was glad. It had been an important year for both of them.

"How do you feel, Rennie?" she heard from class-mates who came up to her all day. "Got the bug?" "You look great!"

She wondered where Lee was and why she hadn't seen him and how could someone be swallowed up so completely in this school when they wanted to be.

Bess picked her up at history class and they went together to archery. Perhaps she would see him there.

She had just shot her first arrow when Lee walked across the field, and next to him, her hand tucked in his elbow, was Jo. Rennie felt sick. Her face flushed in the afternoon sun, and the bow shook.

"Hey," her coach cautioned. "You'll never hit a target with that unsteady hand."

"You're right." Rennie tightened her aim, steadying herself. "Only the lionhearted," she muttered to her-self over and over, as Jo's chatter came closer and closer.

"Hi, Rennie." Jo came over to her right away, a vic-tory smile on her face. "How's archery?"

"Fine. Just fine," Rennie answered. Her mouth felt like chalk. She had only one consolation when it came to Jo. She always knifed her with equality, just as she would have any other competition. There was a mixed feeling of comfort in that.

Lee waved but didn't come over. Jo watched her for a while, watched the arrows fly crazily through the air as if they dropped from the sky, without aim, with-out skill. And then she left.

"Did she come over to kick you in the gut?" Bess asked later.

"Just about," Rennie answered. The day had been a long one. She was ready for it to end. At last her mother's car pulled up, and she felt she was watching a movie flashback, just as it was in the beginning, with Lee and Jo, and now her mother becoming her chauf-feur again. Only Bess was different now. Only Bess had come into the picture and stayed.

She ate little that night. "Rennie," her mother said at last, "I want to say something to you." She wiped her hands on her apron and sat down.

Rennie pushed away her plate. If it was about another doctor, she'd throw the plate against the wall. She wouldn't be able to stop herself. "I've been thinking about what you said the other day. Rennie, all this time that I wanted to spare you from being hurt." She looked down and then stiffened her shoulders, for it had to be said. "Well, I know now I was hurting you, myself. This thing about your walking, about my not accepting the doctor's verdict, of my not accepting"—she paused—"you. Rennie, sometimes I think you adjusted to everything so much better than your father or I did. Could you be a little more patient with us until we catch up?"

Rennie felt fatigue spread through her body. So much to be said, so much to learn, so much to change. She wheeled over to her mother and kissed her.

"Mom," she said, "it's OK. It'll all be OK."

Then she wheeled into her room, and before she put out the lights she reread Carol's letter.

Rennie,

My heart broke for you. I know sometimes I don't seem to believe in anything. Sometimes I don't think I do. But what you were trying to do was the toughest thing of all. If you had won, I guess all of us in wheelchairs would have won a little. You know what I mean? I've found out through the years, you can be treated by those who walk as friends, as confidantes, as a project. But when you talk about love, you talk about crossing over that fine line. And that's when the picture changes. That's when "invalid" and "cripple" become words you begin to hear and have to explain. It's for the best, Rennie. You would have been trying to keep up with him all

*his life and yours, too. I don't know what love is,
but sometimes I think people feel you have to
stand to be part of it. Keep going, Rennie.*

Carol

Rennie turned out the light and looked outside. The
stars were out, and they made checkerboards across
the lawn. A small rabbit, silhouetted in the moonlight,
sat still on its haunches in the silence of the night.
The trees, covered with foliage, had a low music of
their own as the night wind gently moved them against
one another.

Perhaps Carol was right. But never to believe that
love could be strong enough to build a bridge—she
couldn't accept Carol's beliefs as a way of life, either.
Rennie closed the drapes and slid into bed. She'd just
have to find her own way.

The Lionhearted

It was June, a week away from graduation. It had been a month since Lee and Rennie had spoken. Lee saw Rennie every day, from afar. Sometimes he could hear her wheelchair traveling down the halls, sometimes their eyes would meet. There were moments when he longed to walk over to her, to enter that circle that had given him so much during the past months. But he would walk the other way. He had convinced himself that it was better for her. Everything she had said that day at the lake had been true. He had pressured her to stand on those braces, under the pretext that it was the best thing for her. He couldn't forgive himself for that.

So he had decided that she would be better off without him. She was great, great as she was. Someone else would see it. He had seen it. But he had tried to change her, perhaps because he was less of a person than she deserved. During the past slow, colorless weeks, he knew something else. His days weren't the same. There was an emptiness about them that clung to every hour and kept him from sleeping during the long nights.

He and Jo sat near the lake now, and his thoughts,

stubborn and defensive, loyally followed Rennie. He remembered the day he and Rennie had fallen in the lake and how they had laughed afterward. How swift she was in the water, how beautiful her body looked glistening across the lake.

Today was different. There were no clouds, and the sun was hot. The swans were still there, but it wasn't the same. With Rennie, the swans had been brilliantly beautiful, the day exquisite.

"What are you thinking about?" Jo lay on her belly, a long sliver of grass hanging from her mouth.

"I don't know." Lee lay back, his hands under his head. "Just thinking."

"You're thinking it's not the same, aren't you?"

He sat up. She had jolted him with her perception.

"What's not the same?"

"Us. These last couple of weeks." She looked at him and her pretty mouth was set, resigned. "That son of a gun won after all," she said. "Do you know what my trouble was, Lee? I never considered her competition until it was too late."

He knew that she was talking about Rennie. She saw through him. It was true. During these past weeks, wherever his body was, his thoughts had never left Rennie.

He shrugged. "I think you're making too much of it."

She tossed her head and turned away from him. "Tell me you're not thinking of her now."

He wasn't going to lie. He had done enough of that to himself already. There was a silence between them that grew embarrassing.

"Come on." She got up and dusted off her shorts.

"Look," he tried to explain, "what do you want me to say?" He slipped his arm around her waist in a vain attempt to avoid the truth, but she pulled it away.

"It's not fun anymore with you. Nothing's fun anymore. You walk around with those sad cow eyes, and that gets dull after a while." She was ending it. He felt a relief sweep over him.

They walked up the hill toward the car, their arms barely touching. She knew every inch of his body, as he knew hers, and yet they didn't know each other at all. How did he lose his soul to Rennie without even touching her? He dropped Jo off at her home.

"So long," she said. "See you in school." It was over.

She shut the door behind her and didn't look back. One door shut—and one to open. Lee went home. The house was empty.

He ate a sandwich and drank a glass of milk, then sat at the kitchen table, alone with his thoughts. Yet he didn't feel alone at all. He felt Rennie was right by his side. He had felt that way sometimes when he was sorting the ties or waiting on customers, or after he had spent some time with Mr. Dansick and was riding home at night, passing by her house. She was with him. Secretly, he carried her around inside himself.

Then why had he run away? And why was he still running? Was he so afraid to love her? Today, sitting in the kitchen, which felt empty without her, he was more afraid than ever of losing her.

He heard the key in the lock. His mother came in, carrying some bags and out of breath.

He got up and helped her carry the groceries to the kitchen table. She left the bags unopened on the table and put a light under the coffeepot. He waited for her to settle down.

Lee walked over to the sink and took a drink of water. Then, without turning around, he said quietly, "I love her." The words resounded in the kitchen and seemed to echo off the walls. The room was silent, except for the bubbling coffeepot at his elbow.

He turned around, wondering if she had heard him, and understood what he was trying to say. His mother was sitting there, her eyes covered with her hands, her head shaking back and forth as though she were shaking his words off her.

"I know how you feel," he said, and went over to her and put his hand on her shoulder. "I know all the obstacles and all the reasons why it shouldn't be. But there's one good reason why it hangs together. We've never talked about that reason." He sat down so that they were looking at each other. "I love her." He said it aloud and was surprised that the words seemed so at home on his lips. "I love Rennie," he said again, and saying it gave him a thrill of happiness that he had never felt before. He wanted to share it with Rennie right away.

His mother looked away. "I can't make you understand," she said.

"Why won't you understand?" he answered.

This was the point of breaking away for both of them. He could feel the threads snapping, and he didn't know how he could make it less painful. His mother sat in front of him, drinking her coffee slowly.

"You know," he said, wanting to soothe her, "I've never been happier."

Still, she didn't look up.

"I'd like you to meet Rennie's parents, Mr. and Mrs. Jackson. They're great people."

She nodded silently. He knew she would go along with him, perhaps reluctantly, but she would go along. She would only go halfway, if that, and it would be a pity that Rennie would probably never know the woman he had lived with and loved all these years.

"There's nothing I can say to stop you," she said at last. And then, frantically, she added, "If your father were alive . . ." She stopped the words in midair. She didn't have the strength for another battle.

Neither did he. He put her grocery order away, folded the bags and put them in the storage room. Before today, this kitchen, this house had seemed like his home. But now it seemed like his mother's place, her home, and he looked upon it as part of his past.

"Where are you going?" she asked. The answer was in his eyes.

She didn't get up as she usually did to lock the door behind him. He drove around the neighborhood for a while. What if she won't have me? he thought. What if I've waited too long? What if I disappointed her in a way she can't forgive?

Maybe she feels she's better off without me. He drove past the school. He had tried so hard to drive her way. What if he had succeeded? Past Bess's house and the beauty shop.

He pulled into Rennie's driveway and turned off the motor. The house was filled with lights, as though it were waiting for him. He sat in the car, knowing Rennie was close by, inside, and that his knocking on that front door might change both of their lives.

Once more he sorted out his thoughts. He knew the responsibility of what he had to do. He knew he didn't dare take Rennie halfway to nowhere again. And then the words came out in the car, defying all logic. "I love you, Rennie Jackson," he said, and he got out of the car and knocked on the front door.

Mrs. Jackson opened the door. Her face reflected her pleasure when she saw him.

"Hi," he said.

"Hello, Lee, come in." Her voice was warm. "Rennie," she called. "It's Lee. Will you excuse me, Lee? I'm on the phone. Rennie will be right there." She left the room, and he stood there by the door, shifting from one foot to the other.

Rennie wheeled into the room. Standing there, he realized that he had missed her eyes more than anything. He had forgotten how green and deep they were. Looking into them now, he wondered how he could have fooled himself into thinking he could make it without her.

"Look, I'm not going to mess around saying it." He

knelt down by the chair, so that they were face to face. "I was mixed up about this thing"—he pressed against the arms of the wheelchair—"and I'll probably need more straightening out. Would you be willing to take on the education of a guy who is a little disabled when it comes to his thinking?" He took a breath and without letting her say anything he went on. "I don't know what tomorrow holds, Rennie, but neither does anyone else. That sort of makes us all even, doesn't it? It's just that you mean so much to me." He held back. He didn't want to say too much. He stood up and waited.

"What are you saying?" Rennie looked up at him.

He hesitated, then smiled. "I think I'm asking you to go out with me Friday night, to dinner and maybe a movie. How about it?"

She wanted to take him in her arms, because she knew the moment was difficult for him. If there was a line, he hadn't made her cross over. He was crossing over to her. He stood there, just looking at her, waiting for her answer.

"Yes, yes, I'd love to," she said, her face pale, drained by emotion.

He started to leave.

"Wait," she said. "What's the attire for the night?"

"Come as you are," he said and walked over to her. "Exactly as you are." He bent down and kissed her on the lips. He didn't want to stop.

"See you Friday," he said, and closed the door behind him. She heard the motor start in the driveway and the roar of the engine fading down the street.

That night Rennie sat in front of the mirror and stared at herself very hard. She looked like the Rennie she had known two years ago, the one who dared anything, who felt the days were flying by into beautiful tomorrows. She couldn't wait until tomorrow to tell Bess, and to see Lee.

But before she went to bed there was one more

thing she had to do. She opened her box of stationery, took out a pen and a piece of paper. She slid up on the bed, not really believing that it had happened. She was Rennie again. Finally, after two years, they had let her be herself again.

She fell asleep with the stationery in her hand, and the pen on the blanket. All that she wrote was

Dear Carol,

A coach once told me a story about a lion

About the Author

HARRIET MAY SAVITZ is a woman who cares about many things, and her writing is a direct result of her interests. Her most recent novels, including THE LIONHEARTED, reflect her most important concerns. As she herself says, her books are "about the physically disabled, about the change in attitude amongst the disabled population. They're about people of courage who want the rights long kept out of their reach . . . the rights of transportation, accessibility, education, social acceptance, and understanding."

Harriet Savitz travels with the wheelchair sports team, is a member of Disabled in Action, and cofounder of Veep, an organization to help and inform the disabled. She lives with her husband and two children in Plymouth Meeting, Pennsylvania.